Advance praise

"Sizzles with heat, sparkles with charm...you'll savor every sexy, emotion-packed moment!"
— Julie Anne Long, USA Today best selling author of the Hellcat Canyon series

"Fun and flirty, EARNING IT is a winner!"
— Avery Flynn, *USA Today* best selling author of *The Negotiator*

"Get ready to swoon hard for a Navy SEAL! Angela Quarles' first contemporary romance is hot and funny and delivers everything I want in a sexy read. This series is a feast of military and sports heroes—the best possible combination for romance readers!"
— Ainsley Booth, *USA Today* bestselling author of *Prime Minister*

"Sweet and steamy, Earning It is a super fun take on the mistaken identity theme set against an unusual sports romance backdrop. A great read!"
— Kate Meader, *USA Today* bestselling author of the Hot in Chicago series

"Pepper and Luke sizzle...my e-reader almost caught fire during a few sexy scenes. This read was sweetness and smolder with just the right dash of swoon. Whip-smart writing and sly humor abounds-simply my favorite kind of read! Angela Quarles is an up-and-coming contemporary romance writer to watch." — Lia Riley, author of the Off the Map and Hellions Angels series

"...a beautiful feel good romance..."
— Keeana with Bookalicious Babes Blog

ALSO BY ANGELA QUARLES

As You Wish
Steam Me Up, Rawley

Must Love series
Must Love Breeches
Must Love Chainmail
Must Love Kilts
Must Love More Kilts

Stolen Moments series
Earning It

To Valerie!
Enjoy a trip through wacky Florida! :)
Angela Quarles

Risking it

ANGELA QUARLES

Unsealed
ROOM PRESS

This is a work of fiction. Names, characters, places, and incidents either are the product of the author's imagination or are used fictitiously. Any resemblance to actual events, locales, or persons, living or dead, is purely coincidental, except where it is a matter of historical record.

RISKING IT
Copyright © 2017 Angela Trigg
Developmental editing by Gwen Hayes
Line editing by Erynn Newman
Copy editing by Julie Glover
Cover photography: Wander Aguiar
Cover design: Sara Eirew
Cover model: Steven Dehler

Unsealed Room Press
Mobile, Alabama

All rights reserved. Printed in the United States of America. This book or any portion thereof may not be reproduced or used in any manner whatsoever without the express written permission of the author except for the use of brief quotations in a book review.

First Print Edition

To those who love a good road trip

1

JANE

"A DILDO?" THE offending object slips from my fingers and plops onto the carpet floor with a hard, rubbery bounce. I slap my hands over my mouth to stifle my shriek. The smell of plastic coats my fingers which—ack—reminds me what my hands were touching, so I shove them away. I may even be flapping them in the air.

A few library patrons stare quizzically.

"Did I shout that out? Please tell me I didn't shout that out." The Reference Desk where I work is on the second floor, and those staring are on the far side, but *still*. The Selby Public Library has a vaulted ceiling capping the center, which rises two stories. Voices *carry*.

My bestie Claire smirks. "You didn't shout it out." She stoops, picks up the…thing, and holds it out as if she's passing an innocuous baton. But it's not an innocuous baton. It's a dang dildo.

A bright red one too.

Jeez-oh-man.

"Put that away," I whisper fiercely and wipe my hands on my shirt.

I'm not a prude, but this is a family library, for Pete's sake. Where I *work*.

Okay, maybe I'm a smidge of a prude, because honestly?—I stare at what she's holding—that's the first time I've ever touched one. Sure, I've read about them in my racier books, but, you know, my fingers get the job done well enough, thank you very much.

She laughs and drops it back into the liquor box she packed so prettily for me. Complete with red metallic paper and a white fabric bow.

The *thing* lands with a dull *thunk*.

"Claire, what the hell?" I snatch up The Rules—*also* pulled from the box—because there'd been no mention of a dildo. Or even getting off. I think I'd remember that. I flip to the second page of the printout. I mean, she's my bestie and all, but this is ridiculous.

I don't know why I'm shocked though—Claire's never held back. She's tough, and she doesn't care what anyone thinks. Like right now, she's wearing her workout clothes, her hair up in a messy ponytail. Because I know her schedule, I know she's come straight from the Sarasota Sailing Squadron where she works.

"That's your symbolic prop." She met me at the end of my shift and presented me with this Box of Doom. Inside, I found a blank journal, a box of colored pens, a map, and a vintage Polaroid camera. There's even a package of Polaroid film.

"My what?" I lower the pages.

She pushes her fingers onto the top of the The Rules. "Under rule number one. Part b."

I go back and read that subsection again. And groan.

She leans against the Reference Desk and crosses her arms. "You need to get over him."

"Who?" I say with as much nonchalance as I can muster. There's got to be a loophole.

"Don't play dumb. This whole road trip, with *all* the stops, has two purposes: one." She holds up a finger. "To push you out of your shell—"

"My shell?" I toss The Rules into the box.

She waves a hand in front of me, seeming to encompass my cream skirt with ruffles on the hem and sky blue top. "You're hiding behind a stereotype."

"What?"

"The introverted librarian? C'mon, Jane."

I cross my arms. "There's a reason we introverted book nerds flock to these jobs."

"Doesn't mean you can't live a little."

The replacement for my Tuesday half-shift strolls up, and I grab the box. Yes, the embarrassing item's in there. Whew.

"Yep. So you're going on this road trip, my friend."

I crumple the wrapping paper and ribbon and toss it in the trash can. Then I grab my messenger bag and the box and nod to the break room. Claire's met me enough times at the end of my shift to understand. I have no choice. If I want her to reconcile with her mom, I have to do this. That was the pact.

Made one night after too many cocktails.

Ugh. For my first-ever vacation from my first adult job, I'd pick five days of binge-reading in my porch hammock. Not a road trip from Sarasota to Atlanta. With stops at cheesy tourist spots along the way. Just sayin'.

"And two." Up goes another finger as we push into the empty break room.

Oh, right. There were two purposes to this trip.

She rounds on me, her finger still up. She points it at me. "To get over The Turd."

My steps falter. "I'm not hung up on The Turd." I slide the box onto the counter, pushing aside the new literary posters, and open my locker.

The Turd.

That was our nickname so I wouldn't have to say his name. Just thinking about that night together has me flushing with heat. And not the good, sexy kind of heat. Nope. This is the heat of unadulterated embarrassment. Though, to be fair, it was Claire who dubbed him The Turd.

Claire gives me her get-real look.

"Look. I'm fine," I say. "It was one night, that's all. I wasn't expecting more." *Liar*. "And I don't need to do all this soul-searching stuff." I yank the list from the box and wave it to emphasize my point. Yes, I'd been mortified by how much significance I'd given that one night. Even a bit pissed at myself for falling for another charmer. I got over it. Mostly. But… Gawd. The sexual chemistry… I shake off the memories and go back to stuffing some personal items into my bag for this trip she's determined I take.

Honestly, Claire's more upset about that night. She's projecting big time, but I can't prod her about Conor—that hunky Irishman she's *totally* in denial about—without her clamming up.

"Okay." Claire sits at one of the tables and crosses her legs. "Then I don't need to do *my* soul-searching trip." She clasps her hands and rests them on her knee, her sneaker-clad foot arcing back and forth. Looking smug. Damn her.

I snatch The Rules off the counter. How bad can it be?

The worst parts are the stipulations—be at such-n-such spots on such-n-such days. No speeding through and then curling up with a hunky lord in a historical romance.

Then there's documenting the trip in the journal. To, quote, find myself. I roll my eyes. "Can't you pick something different?"

"Hell no." Her foot's now jouncing rapidly. "If I'm taking time out of my life to see that woman"—she makes air quotes—"for my own good, then you have to go through hell too. For *your* own good."

What she has planned, well, except for 1b, would be no sweat for most people. For me, I'd rather… Well, I'd rather be humiliated by The Turd again.

She's set this up brilliantly—made this so unlike me that I'll back out.

But I won't. She really needs to reconcile with her mom. I glance at 1b again, then curl a finger around the edge of the box and tip it closer. I peer inside at the Red Thing.

"Don't worry. He won't be there."

I look at her over my shoulder. "How do you know?"

"I'm captain of the women's team, remember? The men's team is flying out in about an hour."

I can just imagine the impact a plane full of hot male athletes will have on the women flying. I loop my messenger bag over my shoulder and lift the box. "I thought their game wasn't until Saturday?" Dang it. Because *that* didn't reveal anything. Stupid, stupid Jane.

Claire, of course, notices my slip, because she smirks and takes the box from me. "It's not, but they're heading up early. Something about team-building time with their new goalie."

Okay. I take a deep breath. The 1b Rule is now closer to the tolerable end of the scale. I open the door and lead the way out.

I can do this.

Aiden

God*dammit*.

I open the metal panel housing the condenser motor and stare at the fan. The one that should be turning. How can something so simple fuck up everything? Because right now, it's not running the glycol pump. Which means—no tap beer. And we open in forty-five minutes.

Yep. Fucked.

I can't be dealing with this shit right now. I have—I glance at my cell phone on the floor next to the wrench, bolts, and vise grips—less than an hour, tops, before I have to catch a Lyft to the airport. Our hurling team's first, and possibly only, shot at going to the GAA championship in Chicago has it's first hurdle this Saturday in Atlanta—the southeastern division playoffs.

My duffel bag's all packed, sitting in my office, but if I don't get the beer flowing and the bar in the hands of my brand new manager, Stuart, I'm hosed.

Stuart gives me that kind of grin that's like *yeah, we're fucked*, laced with a wobbly *I hope I don't get canned for this*. Even though I think he warned me that the fan was acting wonky.

"Told ya it was making a noise every time it turned off," he says, and now I want to throat punch him.

Which is a strange enough reaction that I slump forward, elbows on my knees. I blow out a sharp breath and grip my hair, hoping the sting will clear my head.

The truth is, my brain's basically mush at this point. Has been for a couple of weeks now. Sleep deprivation will do that to you.

That and a case of blue balls I can't seem to wank away.

I need to get laid. Badly.

Normally, not a problem.

But my body's only wanting one person. Believe me, I've tried. I own a goddamn bar, for fuck's sake. But since that party with Galway New York, when a certain shy book nerd slipped under my skin, it's been pointless.

Which is insane on so many levels. My reputation as a player isn't just smoke and mirrors. I play the field. Constantly. And I love it.

Well, except until recently.

Focus.

I grab my cell again and pull up the Lyft app so it'll be handy.

Fan. I need a new fan. And no time to wait for an electrician. Two years ago, cashing out my share in a San Francisco tech startup, kissing it all goodbye, and using the Florida liquor license I'd won in a poker game to open a bar felt fucking fantastic. Freeing. Too many memories there. Fresh ones to make here in Sarasota. And a chance to fulfill a dream of mine.

Now that dream smells like stale hops, and my palms are sticky from whatever coats the floor in the back of the bar.

I blink dry, scratchy eyes and wipe my palms with a towel. Like any hands-on bar owner, I have vendors on speed dial. I punch the icon for the appliance store over on Orange, leaving a sticky smear on my screen.

"Pete, Aiden here," I say by way of greeting, but I don't have time for niceties, and I'm super-positive most restaurant and bar owners are assholes on a regular basis.

"What's up?" Pete's no-nonsense voice is calming. I tried to get him to play on our hurling team, but he said, being in his forties, he was "getting too old for that shit."

"Need a new condenser fan."

"We close in twelve."

Adrenaline finally—hallelujah—kicks in, clearing away my mental fog. "Can you wait for me? I can switch the fan out myself, but—"

"You gotta open tonight, and you need that fan," he finishes. "I'll wait, but don't lollygag. My little girl has a summer camp thing tonight, and I need to be there."

Relief chases the adrenaline. "Thanks. On my way." I'm already standing, palming my keys, and hoofing it to the back door when it dawns on me. I make a fist against the metal door and stare up at the ceiling. "Fuck!"

"What?" Stuart, who'd been squatting looking at the fan, jumps upright. "Did he not have the part?"

I look at him over my shoulder. How much more can I fuck myself over? "I loaned my goddamn car to Randy."

No sooner are the words out of my mouth than Stuart's tossing me his keys. Maybe this guy'll work out. Besides honesty, knowledge, and experience, the other asset I value in a bar manager is the ability to keep one's cool in a crisis.

Because there's always a crisis, right? And you don't need a manager freaking out, or worse, creating them when there aren't any. You'd be surprised by the number of pot-stirrers in the restaurant industry.

"Be right back." I toss his keys in the air and catch them.

I point to the mess on the floor. "While I'm gone, have that fan unscrewed and out."

Stuart nods. "You got it, boss."

I shove open the door. And kiss my flight goodbye.

Dammit. I fish out my cell to start searching for alternate ways to get to Atlanta.

2

JANE

I DRUM MY fingers on my car's steering wheel, scanning the sidewalk along Lemon, watching everything and everyone like some kind of stalker-freak. Not that there's a crowd out there or anything—it's only five o'clock on a Tuesday.

To complete my stalker-freak ensemble, I'm wearing a cotton beach cover-up with a hood. I timed the frequency with which people wander past this parking lot—odds are I can do this without attracting notice. Not perfect odds, which, yeah, is why I'm stalling, with a hood tugged low over my head.

And I'm clutching the Red Thing as if it's some kind of talisman that will save me.

Trust me. The symbolism is not lost on me.

I rehearse movements so I can keep the visibility of the dildo to a minimum.

How the heck did I get to this point? I'm a friggin' *librarian.* Our tribe doesn't…doesn't do outrageous stuff like this in public. I know it's a cliché that librarians don't like to socialize, but c'mon—what I said to Claire earlier is true. People like me flock to jobs like that. We'd rather be nose deep in a book than at a party.

Which is what got me to this point. Ugh.

Claire invited me to some after-party for her Irish team sport-thing. I'd blocked out that night to binge-read the latest urban fantasy book in my favorite series, but I'd put her off too many times last month. So I went. Mainly because that would give me credit for going.

It was sooo not my scene. A crowded bar. Jocks everywhere. Girls all primped and pretty with shiny lip gloss. Brought it crashingly home that I'm an odd duck, ya know?

And then The Turd approached. We got to chatting. I only had two beers, so I can't blame the alcohol, but as I stared up at this hot guy, the urge to do something completely out of character animated me.

Like find out what my ex-boyfriend found so compelling last year about sleeping with people he had no feelings for.

Sounds great, right? Very pro female, owning my sexual self kind of thing. Go me.

Ha ha.

Yeah.

Fresh humiliation washes through me—how pathetic that I'd set out to play with a player and he didn't even want to play.

I wanted to shrivel up and die that morning.

"Maybe you were right, Claire," I whisper. Maybe I am more hurt about that night than I thought.

I shove the dildo into a brown paper bag I unearthed in the mess of my back seat.

Rule 1b doesn't specify *what* I have to do, but it must be symbolic and make a statement. And be done at The Turd's parking lot.

Let's do this. I grab the Bic and lighter fluid I bought at the Walgreens on the way here. What suspiciously feels like glee trips through me. What the heck?

Okay, maybe I *do* need to get out more.

Whatever. But dang, it sure feels like I'm in the middle of a Bridget Jones book.

I snag the bag with the rest of my supplies and slip out of the car. I waited until his flight left before heading over.

Just to be sure. He's the last person I want to see. Especially with what I plan.

I scurry across The Alligator's Butt parking lot, my heart beating as furtively as my movements. I choose a section near the dumpster, because this excursion is all about The Symbolism, right? Screw Claire.

So anyway, I head there and plop my butt onto the cement curb in front of an empty parking spot near enough to my chosen spot.

I pull out all my supplies—except the dildo—so they're readily accessible.

The film's already loaded, and I tested the camera. It works. Yay.

Not.

I scribble a soul-searching passage in the journal about what I'm doing, and why, and what I hope to gain from it.

Burning the dildo in effigy. Looking forward to seeing it burn.

Hey, she neglected to specify length of entries, okay? Also, there's a godawful stench coming from the dumpster. I want to keep this short.

Not that I'd have expounded otherwise. It's a convenient excuse, though, in case Claire quibbles. As a token effort of getting into the spirit of the journey, I fish out the red pen and draw some hearts around the journal entry.

I hold the journal out, tilt my head, and nod. Looks good. I stuff the journal into my messenger bag, along with the pens.

A couple walks past, but they're so lovey-dovey, they don't notice me. Honestly, someone sitting by a bar dumpster is probably not a weird sight in downtown Sarasota, so I have that going for me.

But I wait until they disappear from view and then peer sideways at the paper bag.

Nothing for it.

I yank the Red Thing out and toss it onto the pavement, where it bounces and rolls drunkenly in an arch. Next, I squirt lighter fluid all over that sucker and flip the Bic. I touch the flame to the Red Thing and—*woosh*—I jump back as it flares upward.

Eek!

I nervously eye the pinestraw mulch about a foot away, but the flame quickly dwindles to a sickly purple and smoke curls into the air, bringing with it the smell of burning plastic.

As the phallic shape melts and oozes on the pavement, I do an honest-to-God fist pump. It just feels so great. So... okay, *symbolic*.

To comply with 1b, I grab the Polaroid and peep through the hole, lining up a shot. I hit the button, and a flash of light illuminates the ground and the sizzling, burbling effigy, followed by a *kuh-kuh-ntchuhhh* as the floppy rectangle of film ejects.

Suuuuch a weird way to snap a picture.

"What the hell's going on here?"

My heart, I swear to God, compresses to a pinpoint. I *know* that voice.

I've dreamed that voice.

He's not supposed to *be* here.

Aiden

The fuck?

I blink at the scene before me. Some crazy person just lit a fire in the parking lot of my goddamn bar. Can tonight get any more fucked?

I drop the trash and rush over. It's only a whimper of a flame, but with how my day's going, I'm not taking chances.

I squash the flames with my work boots and skid sideways at the gooey slickness. Red, blackened slickness.

What the—?

Behind me, a giggle, quickly stifled, cuts through the air.

Well, that's unexpected—I assumed the slight figure in the hoodie was some young *male* punk.

I spin around. Said *feminine* person's easing one foot back, then another, head down.

Normally, I'm not confrontational, but today's been screwy, and I've fuck-all patience with everyone and everything. If this chick's causing problems on my property, I want to know. And stop it.

"Not so fast." I lunge forward and grab her arm just as she twists to move away. Which causes her hoodie to droop off.

My hand flies off her as if it's been burned. "You!"

The cause of my sleepless nights is right in front of me, ladies and gentlemen. Burning something in my parking lot. Because my day can't get any more fucked.

Jesus.

I haven't seen her since the morning we parted. Vulnerability leaks from her, making me feel as if I'm handling a hot potato. And handling it badly. Some kind of freaky-weird need washes through me. A need to protect. A need to comfort. I don't like it.

It's daylight, but the sun's low in the sky and she's standing in the one spot that has her partially shadowed by the taller building next door. I can still make out the soft curve of her full lower lip, which contrasts with her narrow upper one. For some reason, the disproportionateness (is that a fucking word?) slays me. I've definitely had wicked-hot visuals cycle through my mind of those lips doing—

I wrench away from *that* inevitable path, because my damn dick is getting ideas.

We're standing in the parking lot like two gunslingers facing off. At least she's not darting off. Unlike the night we met, her brown hair's cinched up in a ponytail.

I thumb behind me. "What were you up to?"

Like a turtle going back into its shell, she pulls her hood back up and shoves her hands in her hoodie pockets. It shows how fucking tired I am that I didn't even notice the lace trimming the hem, cluing me in to her gender.

"It's…" She clears her throat. "It's not what it looks like."

Her voice. Goddammit. I am *not* reacting to hearing its tones for the first time in weeks like Pavlov's damn dog.

I glance over my shoulder at the reddish blob as her words finally penetrate. "It looks like you lit something on fire in my parking lot."

"Um. Yeah." She nods her head. "That's what it is. It looks like what it is," she says on a rush, her voice breathless. Eager. Relieved.

Okay. I'm confused, but it could be because I'm operating on zero sleep. Thanks to her. "Why?"

"It was…it was something nasty that, er, needed to be, um, snuffed out so it won't continue…contaminating its surroundings."

She looks up and away, and I'm staring at her profile under the hood, trying to decide if her words make any sense. Remember, my brain is mush.

I go with it. Easier that way. "What're you doing here?" I wince. Jesus, that sounded accusatory, as if she doesn't have a right to be anywhere she damn well pleases. But part of me is like, *why here?*

She twirls her car keys, the metal *clinking* rhythmically. "Actually, I'm about to go on a road trip to Atlanta." She glances at her car. "I need to leave. I thought…I thought you were flying out?"

I'm thrown for a sec that she knows this, until I remember Claire's her best friend.

"I missed my flight." And the ones that'll get me there now will max out my purposely small credit limit.

She stops clinking her keys. "Sorry. That sucks. Driving?"

"Yeah, borrowing a friend's car." And as soon as he gets here, I can take off. The new motor's in place, and the beer's running cold.

"What happened to yours?" *Clink, clink, clink* go her car keys again.

"Loaned it to a buddy since I thought I'd be out of town."

"Can't you get it back?"

I shake my head. "He's already halfway to Miami."

"Oh. Okay. Um, good, er, running into you. Bye." She backs away, avoiding my gaze.

Should I be offended that she wants so little to do with me?

And without a backward glance, she ducks into her car and leaves.

Leaving *me* standing in my parking lot, a bag of trash and a red smear on the ground nearby, and wondering—what the fuck just happened?

Aiden

Thirty minutes later

"You've got to be fucking kidding me."

I'm staring at the steam shooting from the hood of my friend's car. I kick the tire, which feels all kinds of satisfying but doesn't do a damn thing about getting me to Atlanta.

I managed to pull the car into a nearby gas station off Fruitville road. I guess I should be happy it happened before I got on the interstate, right? I pull out my cell and type:

```
Your car died. Sorry.
```

I then shoot him my GPS location.

```
Shit. Sorry. Leave it there
until I can figure out what
to do.
```

Now what the hell am *I* going to do?

Tires crunch behind me, along with the buzz of a window lowering.

"Aiden?"

I close my eyes. *No.* It can't be.

"You okay?" Jane's voice is louder, as if I hadn't heard her.

I whirl around. Her window's down, and she's looking up at me, her forehead creased.

"Hey." I run my hands through my hair.

She drapes an arm on her door and pokes her head out. "What happened?"

"Car's radiator blew." I take in the sight of my buddy's car, which is now just a steaming pile of junk. I pivot back at Jane. In her car.

My tired mind coughs up an idea. It's stupid, and I'm now questioning my sanity. The truth is, she blew me off. I told myself I was relieved. And I *am.* Though if I dig down enough, I know it bothers me. There's something else though too, besides irritation and relief. It's…who the fuck knows? But maybe now I can find out. Find out why she left and find out what else this reaction is.

"You're going to Atlanta?"

Her head tucks back into the car's interior. "Yeeesss…"

I step forward. "Take me with?"

Her eyes widen with panic, but I can tell she's trying to straddle the politeness line. "Can't you rent a car?"

"All booked." At least all the cheap ones were. It's why I'd resorted to borrowing this car.

Now her arm comes off the window, and she's completely in the shadow of her car. "I… It's not a straight shot."

Her voice is hard to hear, so I close the distance and lean toward her with my hand propped against the car's roof. "Not a straight shot?"

She shakes her head. "I won't get there until Friday. I'm leaving now, but I'm taking a roundabout way."

Friday'll get me there in time for the game. This team-building stuff is bullshit. The team wants me there early, and I can still catch that expensive flight, but I'm peeved that it'll cost me so much. Especially on top of the unexpected repairs tonight. Even if I pay for the gas on this trip and take into account hotel stays, it'll be waaay cheaper.

She starts rambling about how tedious and boring it'll be, and I'm fighting both annoyance and a smile. She's really doing her damnedest to unsell this trip, and it's having the opposite effect.

Perversely I want to do the exact opposite of what she wants here.

"I'm in."

Her face drains of color. "But…but…"

I hit her with my sure-fire, panty-melting smile. It's kind of unfair, but… "Please? You'll be doing me a solid."

And maybe I can find out why the hell she ghosted me after we had such an awesome night together.

"It'll be *boring*!" she says in desperation.

Boring? Music to my ears. A boring car ride with this woman might be just the method to work her out of my system.

3

Jane

This can*not* be happening.

So. Yeah. Here's me heading out on this stupid soul-searching road trip. It was bad enough that I got caught fulfilling 1b in The Rules by Aiden, aka The Turd.

This is a friggin' nightmare. The Turd is leaning against my car, all easy charm, and…and…batting his ridiculously long eyelashes, and…

Okay, he's not batting his eyelashes, but I feel compelled, okay? Just like the night I met him, I'm sucked into his orbit by his charm and can't seem to pull away.

Also, the horrifying, holy shit feeling that he'd caught me *setting fire* to the Red Thing is still right there, pushing against my skin, making me feel both sick and antsy.

He wasn't supposed to be there. And now I pull in to fill up my tank and find him stranded. The universe is having a laugh.

Here's the thing—I know he's a playboy. There can never be more with him. But tell that to my body. It just up and goes *hey there* as soon as he gets close, completely ignoring the fact that he's absolutely the wrong kind of guy to get involved with, much less that he just caught me burning an effigy of a penis.

Charmers like him are fun for others to play with, but I've been let down too many times by men like him.

I have a weakness for them, though I never realize their nature *at the time*. The boogers sneak up on me. Case in point—it took me until I caught my ex-boyfriend Brett cheating on me to see that side. I'm getting better at spotting them, but Aiden proves I still suck at it. Once I found out he was a player, I dropped the connection. Fast.

Claire's wrong—I don't need to find myself. I already know I'm the type that's better off alone. Because the kind of relationship I want—dedicated to each other and equal partners and a good dose of passion—well, let's face it, I'm not the outgoing, va-va-voom type that can attract a guy like that.

My forecast of what I can expect? Some nice guy who seems safe and compatible, and then cheats on me after we have kids. Nope.

I wasn't even enough to inspire the one-night stand I wanted with him. How pathetic is that? For the first time, I pick up a guy and nothing happens. The whole night. Nothing.

"Please," he says again.

Gah. He's batting those lashes now. He was clean-shaven the night I met him, but now his strong jaw has a five o'clock shadow, which being blond gives him a bit of an edgy look. Couple that with his straight nose, prominent cheekbones, and those languid eyes, it's like he's deploying weapons to slay me.

This trip is partly because of *him*. A trip I'd rather not do. Journaling. Traipsing around tourist sites. The night we met, I was standing by a post in the crowded bar while Claire was playing darts with Conor but pretending like she had no interest in him whatsoever.

Nearby, two guys were chatting, and yeah, I picked the spot to hang with Claire because the dark-haired one was kinda cute. Slightly dorky, with glasses. My speed. I didn't plan to act on it though. No way.

And then the *friend* approached. Who was not at all my type. For one thing, he was blond. But he was also one of the muscular, good-looking types that, while I can objectively acknowledge why girls—and some guys—would fan themselves on sight, have just never done it for me. Too hunky.

More to the point, I'm not their type. So I figured he was smoothing the way for his shy friend. But when he came within a foot or so, I became a firm believer in pheromones. Up till then, the concept had been theoretical to me. But, holy cow, when he stepped within my space and started talking, *everything* inside me perked up. And tingled.

Which was such a novelty that it took me a moment to realize he *wasn't* there for his friend. And all that tingling morphed into nervous excitement and swooped right into my stomach.

And it's doing it again. My stomach. Being all swoopy. Shit.

Telling him *why* I can't have him along on this trip would be admitting too much. Shit. And he's stranded. And we're going to the same place.

I grip the steering wheel, pull in a deep breath to ground myself, and say, "Sure."

Aiden

Relief sweeps through me at Jane's words. Relief I don't want to examine. "Don't leave."

She thumbs behind her. "I've gotta get gas. Join me when you're ready."

It's a busy station, so she pulls in behind another car to wait her turn while my sluggish brain works through the next steps. My buddy's got a spare set of keys, so that's easy.

I text him an update and hotfoot it to the trunk. Next, I tap Luke's number on my cell and snag my duffel bag. I texted him earlier about missing my flight.

"Hey, man. Bad news." I fill him in on my itinerary. I'm calling him instead of Conor, our captain, because it was Luke's idea to get up to Atlanta so damn early.

"We need you up here before Friday." In the background I can hear a loudspeaker announcement, so they must've just landed.

"Not really. It's the defense that needs the extra team-building with the new goalie."

Luke sighs through the phone. "I don't like this. We're supposed to be a team."

"We *are* a team." There's an edge to my voice. The resentment's been building since they first proposed we take extra days off to go up early. "I'll be there Friday. Plenty of time to kick it around with the guys before game-time Saturday."

I lock up, and Luke's still talking. "I could talk to Conor about using the sponsorship funds to pay for your flight." They paid for the one I missed. I can't ask them to fork over more.

Jane's still waiting, so I park my ass on the hood. "No. I...I need this." And, fuck, I'm not lying. I'm exhausted. My whole world's been this damn bar, the training for the playoffs, and lately, angsting over Jane.

The way I see it, this trip can help with all three—get Jane out of my system and give me space from the bar and the team to regain my equilibrium. And the idea of driving up there tonight was about more than my brain could take.

Luke's not happy as he talks through the rest of the logistics with me, but I can't seem to care.

"Who's giving you a ride again?"

"A friend of Claire's."

"A friend of Claire's?" No way he knows what happened—he wasn't at the after-party due to an injury—but his voice has a trace of suspicion. "The one you hooked up with?"

Fuck. "I didn't hook up with her." At least not in the

way he thinks.

"Then don't hook up with this one either. Keep your dick holstered, all right? We don't need the drama with the women's team."

I push off the car. "Fuck you, Luke."

"I'm serious. Normally I wouldn't give a shit, but if it affects the team…"

It's always about the team with him. I roll my eyes.

He's still going. "…sooner or later you've gotta stop being a man-whore. I know getting left at the altar by your college sweetheart messed you up, but—"

Oddly, humiliation flares that I'd thought long fucked away. "Jesus, you guys are the worst gossips. Who told you that?"

"Does it matter?"

Jane's pulling up at the pump. "Look, I've gotta go. I'll send updates. See you on Friday." I hit end before he can reply. Just because Luke's got something permanent doesn't mean it's right for me. Fucking love peddler.

Jane

Finally, the line moves, and I pull up at the pump. Which means I have to tear my gaze from the rearview mirror and Aiden. Weak. I'm so weak. I mean, what the hell? How is having Aiden on this trip going to help me get over him?

Wait. I don't need to get over him. My life's perfectly fine, and it's Claire who's reading more into it. Claire who thinks I need to get over him. Silly Claire.

I unlatch the seat buckle and catch movement on the passenger side. Aiden fishes his wallet from his back pocket, and his butt—okay, his *muscular* butt—is framed by the window, his jeans molding to him perfectly. He, thank God, doesn't wear his jeans so low they're falling off. His are in that wonderful range where they're snug enough to show he actually *has* a butt, but not so tight he's in danger of cutting off circulation and looking douchey.

It really is a nice butt. Firm. Grippable.

Wow, okay. It's not just Claire being silly. It's also my stupid libido.

He doesn't want you, okay?

Then it hits me what he's doing, and I launch out of the car. "I've got this!"

He glances at me over the top of the car. "Nope." He swipes his card. "You're driving. I'm paying."

I narrow my eyes. Too late now, but, gah, I don't like that he's paying for my gas.

He completely ignores my narrow-eyes. "So what's our first stop?" Behind him, the gas filling the tank *clicks* along, marking time.

I sigh. "Solomon's Castle."

Now *he* does the narrow-eyes thing, though his has a hint of tease, like he's throwing it back at me. "You don't seem too excited."

Shit. Can't have him pry into who was behind this. Or why. I paste on a smile. "I am! Just tired." I cross my arms over the roof and plant my chin on my forearm. I stifle a yawn to lend authenticity.

"Need me to drive?"

"Oh! Uh, no. I'm not *that* tired." God, I sound like the biggest idiot.

He stares a moment longer, like he's totally seeing through my BS. The *clunk* of the gas shutting off startles us both. He taps the nozzle and replaces it.

"I'm gonna get a Coke Zero," I say. "Want anything?"

He shakes his head. "I'm good. I might, er, nap, if that's cool with you?"

I nod like a friggin' maniac, because yeah, that'd be awesome. No pressure. No worrying about conversation topics. No awkwardness about That Night.

I make a pit stop while I'm inside, because it's always good to empty the tank, and on the way out I nab my Coke Zero. A small bag of Funyuns beckons from an end-cap display. I grin like some Disney villain hatching a plot—nothing says *I have no plans to hook up with you* more than Funyun breath. I throw those suckers on the counter too.

Back at the car, Aiden's pushing the seat as far back and as low as it can go.

He looks up as I get in the car, and I give him a nod and a smile like I'm totally cool, totally the type of girl who goes on road trips with hot guys all the time. No biggie. Mm-hmm. I stash my drink and snack in the center and pull out of the station, heading east. He takes no notice of my snack statement. Jerk.

In fact, he just closes his eyes and crosses his arms across his very broad chest. Jeez, they take up the whole width of the seat. This car's too small for the both of us.

As we tool out Fruitville road, his breaths even out. The little faker. He's totally not asleep.

What—he can't just hang with me? He has to fake sleeping to escape me?

Holy shit. I'm annoyed. How annoying! Which makes me snort.

But soon he's conked out for real. How do I know? Because I glance over at a soft snore, and his face is relaxed and peaceful, his mouth slightly open. His lips are full in a unique way that makes me want to nibble on them—the bottom one slightly puffy *below* the actual lip, like a shelf to support his lip. Or like it's swollen from a fight. Or kissing. Sounds weird, but it works on him. Part of the hot, chiseled look he's got going on.

Relaxed like this, the half circles on each side of his mouth are gone too.

My stomach does this weird little flip, because he's so gorgeous but also so vulnerable, and I don't know what to do with that.

And then I shake myself.
Nothing.
I do *nothing* with that.
I do nothing with *him*.

4

Aiden

I JOLT AWAKE, not sure why. Then I realize it's the silence and the stillness. I blink my memory back into place. Oh yeah. Car trip. To Atlanta. I sit up and—*ouch*—bang my knee on the dashboard.

I rub it. Brain catching up.

...A car trip with Jane. Who's not in the driver's seat.

It's nearing dusk, and we're parked on the side of the road. An isolated, tree-lined road. She must have pulled off of the interstate for some reason. I look at my cell. While it feels like longer, it's only been twenty minutes since we left the station.

Where the fuck is she?

I scan out the windshield, my heart beating a bit faster as my brain crowds with all these wild-ass, horror-movie scenarios.

"Looking for me?" an amused voice says right behind me, which, I hate to admit, makes me give out an unmanly, shall we say, squeak?

She's in the back, a journal open in her lap. Colored pens are lying in the indentations of the seat, and she's taping a Polaroid pic onto a blank page.

I look out the back window. The pic is of the sun setting

behind us, but from about ten minutes prior.

I know this'll sound weird, but seeing her journaling—something so serious and *earnest*—is a welcome bucket of cold water over me. Before I fell asleep for real, I thought I'd fucked myself over. Smelling her sweet scent, hearing the little noises she made, like humming the first lines of each song and stopping as it cycled through her playlist, was making me *more* aware of her.

This trip is supposed to cure me.

But seeing this? Yeah, she's a serious woman, a reader, an intellectual. She'd want to be with a serious guy who could get into this kind of stuff with her, share philosophical insights on life and all that crap.

We're not right for each other, chemistry notwithstanding. Even if I was looking for a relationship. Which I'm not.

Luke said, *"Stop being a man-whore,"* but that's my comfort zone. I'm not cut out for relationships.

Fucking Luke.

Fucking lot of gossipers. Who told him about Brittany anyway?

I face forward and drop my head back against the seat, closing my eyes.

It's pathetic, right? I stood there, with my best man beside me, my family and all my friends in that stupid church and *waited*. At first, I made excuses. She had a wardrobe malfunction and would be out any minute.

She was trying to get her hair *just right*.

The photographer was holding her up with all the pre-ceremony pics.

One of her bridesmaids came down with the stomach flu.

The kicker? I was convinced it was one thing or another holding her up.

I was *that* certain Brittany would be walking down the aisle to start her life with me. We'd talked about this moment since nearly the beginning of college.

I was such a clueless idiot.

Of course, it eventually penetrated my thick skull.

I'd been left at the altar.

All I got was a text—the next day, mind you—that simply said: *I'm sorry.*

Like that fucking helped.

I'm sorry I can't go through with this?

I'm sorry you weren't what I wanted?

I'm sorry I met some other dude?

I never did find out why. At first I wanted closure, and then I didn't care. I vowed never again to be a damn doormat in a relationship. The Mr. Nice Guy.

Too much work and not worth the effort.

So yeah, seeing Jane like this? It clicks into place that odd feeling of relief I'd felt when she blew me off. Deep down I knew, despite how well we hit it off and how attracted we were to each other, this would never work out.

I *did* make the right call to beg a ride. I'm on the road to recovery.

Now I need to find out why she ditched me. It's an unresolved thread.

Aiden

A CAR DOOR *thunks* closed, and I jerk awake. The car's stopped. It's dark, though a sickly glow of light makes me squint. I blink and sit up. Jane's disappearing through an automatic door into what I'm guessing is a hotel, judging by the architecture, the lobby, and the curved driveway in front.

I stretch and roll my neck. Sleep's fogginess edges away by degrees. Fuck, I must've been conked out. I *said* I wanted to nap, but I didn't think I *would. Twice.* Not when the reason for my sleeplessness was in the damn car.

Jesus, I'm slacking. I push open the door. The hotel's one

of those moderately priced chains with the rooms inside, so I grab her suitcase and my bag and follow.

No one else is in line, so I sidle up next to her just as the clerk slides across one key card.

Oh, hell no.

"Er, I don't think that's a good idea." Cuz, yeah, that sleep not only cleared my brain fog, it also showed how stupid my thought processes were earlier today, thinking this trip would be a cure, journaling notwithstanding. Being near Jane? Bad idea. Even now, in the sterile lobby, I'm feeling a pull. Especially because my body's thinking *hotel room, score!*

She glances up, one eyebrow raised. Of course she can do the one-eyebrow thing. I've tried. Hello, Star Trek fan here. But both of mine just go up, and I look ridiculous.

"What isn't a good idea?" she asks.

I nod at the key card now in her hand. "Sharing a room."

She edges back a step. "Who said we're sharing?"

I'm relieved. I absolutely am. I look down at the key card and back.

She rolls her eyes. "I'm getting my own room. I figure you know how to book—and *pay*—for your own." She grips the handle of her rolling suitcase, nods to the night clerk, and strolls for the elevator, a gotcha-sashay to her walk if I've ever seen one.

"Hey, at least wait up." I don't expect her to, but she stops, turns, and crosses her arms.

Well, okay then. I hand over my credit card and ID to the clerk, who's standing there with a bemused expression. "Can you put us on the same floor?"

"Sure, bud." Not much younger than me, he clicks away with brisk efficiency.

All done, I join her, and we walk in silence to the elevator alcove, the only sound her suitcase wheels rolling across the lobby's laminate flooring.

I thumb the up button and give her a smirk. "Were you going to leave me in the car?"

Her eyes go wide. "The car." She sighs. "Jeez, I'm tired. No,

I planned to wake you, move the car, and grab the luggage. With my luggage in hand, I kinda forgot that part." Her cheeks redden.

Now I feel bad—if I hadn't been so exhausted myself, I could have kept her awake and entertained. "I'll move it after we put our luggage in the rooms." The elevator door dings open. "Which floor?"

"Third." She steps inside, and I follow.

"Ah, me too."

She rolls her eyes again and leans against the far wall. "I heard you ask him, slick."

"Blessed with freakish hearing too. My kind of woman."

She just looks upward and taps her foot until we reach our floor. We exit, glance at our key cards and the directional sign, and turn right down the hall. Sweet. Same wing. Big tip for that clerk.

But then we pause at adjacent doors, and I want to punch him. Dude—near enough to kinda-sorta be protective but not so close that she's on the other side of a fucking wall.

Christ.

I glance sideways—she's avoiding looking at me. Though it takes her three times to work the key card. She curses softly, and I hold the door open so she can maneuver her suitcase inside unimpeded.

She shoves her luggage against the wall and finally looks at me. "You have your own room."

I smile. "I know." I hold out my hand, and she stares at it as if I'm handing her her doom. I bounce my hand. "Keys?"

"Oh, right." Red splotches mark her cheeks. So fucking cute. She fishes around in her purse and drops them into my hand.

I give a nod. "I'll be right back."

I drop my bag off in my room, cursing. What the fuck had I been thinking? What dumb ass gets in a car with a girl he's got the hots for and thinks that it'll make him *not* attracted to her? And I'm damn sure she said we'd take several days too. Fuck.

Calling myself all kinds of stupid as I hoof it downstairs, I park her car in one of the hotel's designated spots.

Soon enough, I'm back at her door. I give a soft rap. She answers but only opens the door a crack, as if it's a shield she's hiding behind, and I hate that she feels that way.

I have no idea what made her blow me off. And, yeah, I'm not used to that. But that's not the point. The point is, I want to know *why*, and it's killing me that I don't.

Her defensive posture, though—Jesus, it's like a punch in the gut. Quickly, I sort through our first night together. A night where for *once* I didn't push to see how far our mutual attraction could take us. We just…watched *Monty Python and The Holy Grail,* and then other fun, campy movies. Laughed. Snuggled. And that's it. If anything, watching movies late into the night under a shared blanket until we fell asleep and *not* making a move should show her I can be trusted.

I don't get it.

So I hold up her keys, which have a die-cast bronze miniature stack of books for a keychain. "You're all set. What time're we starting out?"

"Meet downstairs at eight?" She snags the keys.

"No."

Her eyes widen.

"I'll meet you in this *hallway* at eight."

She gives a shaky nod and starts to close the door. I put a hand to it, and she looks up with a start.

"Night, Jane."

Honest to God, more Zs get added to the sizzle in the air between us. What is it about her? And is it one-sided? I need to stay away, but I want to know the answer to this question more.

She rubs the back of her neck, her gaze holding mine for a full three seconds. And…I think she just flicked her gaze to my lips. I could have missed it, it was so quick. Except I didn't. Cuz I'm watching her closely. So the reason she ghosted me was *not* that she's not attracted to me. I store that tidbit away and step over to my door.

I slip my key card into my door lock, and from the darkness of her door's opening, her whisper emerges. "Night, Aiden." Her door *snicks* shut as mine clicks open.

What the fuck is going on?

My brain must still be fried from lack of sleep. Sure, I was out like a light for a good hour or so, but...

I toss my duffel bag onto the spare double bed and yank open the bag's zipper. Inside, I grab my dopp kit and pad to the bathroom. A good night's sleep—that's what I need.

Teeth brushed, I head out of the bathroom, pulling off clothes. I've got my pants and boxers shoved to my thighs when I stop.

Fuuuuck me. There's an adjoining door. We're not only sharing a wall, but there's a door?

As if my clothes are at fault, I yank the rest off, tripping on a pants leg as I stumble to the bed. Once I'm as naked as a damn jaybird, I wrench back the top sheet and comforter, fall onto the mattress, and grab the remote. Again, as if inanimate objects are to blame, I vengefully jerk the sheet back over me and punch the TV on.

Mindless TV. That should help. I thumb the channel button over and over, looking for anything to take my mind off Jane and the situation I put myself in, but her door. It's right there, at the edge of my vision. Taunting.

Why did I think this was a good idea? Goddamn sleep-deprived, squishy mush of organic matter in my fucking brainpan.

She's right on the other side of the door.

Which I'm staring at instead of the TV.

Probably undressed by now. Does she wear pajamas or shorts and a T-shirt, or...nothing? And if they're pajamas, are they serious ones or goofy ones? Or, Jesus. Sexy ones?

Aaaaand now I'm popping up a tent with the sheet.

Yeah, this is by far the most idiotic idea I've ever had. And that's saying something.

I need a new Plan B.

I launch across the space between the beds and snag my

duffel. I fish out my charger, plug in my cell, and pull up megabus.com. Okay, there's a stop in Tampa. If we haven't passed Tampa, I can ask her to drop me off.

I freeze—where *are* we? Based on the time, we drove for a little over an hour. So straight-up I-75 should put me near Tampa.

I pull up Google Maps. The location dot blinks in…the middle of nowhere? I pan out. What the—? We're not north of Sarasota, but almost directly east. In Arcadia.

Arcadia?

What the hell is in Arcadia? Everyone's familiar with the developed, beachy coastline, but most don't know that sandwiched between those two coastlines? Fucking cow country. Weird, right? That's Florida.

Jane told me the first stop. What was it? Jesus, my mushy brain can't remember.

At some point, we'll need to head north, though, because, *hello*, Atlanta is north. And I know in my sleep-deprived mind I didn't mess up on our ultimate destination.

I don't think.

Fuck me.

Not knowing when I'll be near enough to Tampa to catch the MegaBus, I can't purchase tickets, but I check the times. I'll have to book two separate tickets, but there are several a day.

I fall back onto the bed, relieved. Okay. That's an option. A *doable, sane* option.

I slide back under the sheets, resolved to get off this circuit-jamming road trip ASAP.

5

Jane

At one minute until eight in the morning, I slip out of my room and glance at Aiden's door. Through every fault of my own, I'm stuck with him in my car for the next couple of days. Doesn't mean we have to walk down the hall and share an elevator ride and then breakfast.

So I'm giving Aiden until one minute after and then heading down. My phone screen shows the time morph to 8:00 a.m. I tug on my shirt hem and keep my focus trained on the phone, as if by keeping my attention there—and not on the man's door—it'll magically tick to one minute after without him appearing. And then I'm freeeeeee. Well, free to head downstairs without his hunkiness crowding my space.

Aaand…queue the inevitable fluttery weird feeling whenever even a portion of me is thinking about him.

My phone changes to 8:01. I pump my fist, turn, and stumble. Somehow without me hearing, Aiden's slipped open his door, and his sleep-fuzzy face gives me a tired smile. He steps to my side.

Gah.

So much for getting away with being a chickenshit. "Morning."

"Morning," he responds, and we turn and stroll down

the deserted hallway.

The quiet is all kinds of awkward, and my stomach knots up even more. Performance anxiety.

I mentally slap myself. I'm going about this all wrong. He's not interested. Then so what? Why bother weighing what I say and do in order to "entice" him or some such nonsense. Or worry that I'm as much of a turn-off as he already thinks I am. We're stuck with each other for several days, and it'll become more awkward if we let it.

A weight lifts from my shoulders.

"So what was the fist pump for?" His voice still has the sexy, stubbly sound of sleep.

Jeez-oh-man. "Um. You know, just excited to start the morning."

He scoffs. "No, you're not. I've never seen someone less interested in the start of their own trip."

I straighten and paste on a smile. "I'm excited. I am. This is my…excitement voice and face. Trust me."

He looks at me, both eyebrows raised. "Okay. Recalibrating." He thumbs the down arrow.

"Huh? Never mind. Let's start over. Sleep well?"

He chuckles and leans against the wall. "Yeah." And oddly, his voice is laced with surprise. "So what's on today's agenda? Why are we all the way out in Arcadia?"

I was wondering when he'd realize where we were. The elevator dings, and we step aboard. "After breakfast, we'll head to Solomon's Castle, which is nearby."

His forehead wrinkles. "What's that?" He pushes the button for the lobby.

"I don't know, actually."

He stops rocking back and forth and latches his gaze on mine. "For real?"

God, the full force of his stare is… It's friggin' unnerving. "Yeah."

The *ding* of an incoming text fills the confines of the elevator just as it stops on the second floor. I pull up my phone and move aside for a family of three getting on. It's a text from Claire:

> Hey girl. I want details!
> How'd the penis burning go?

She ends it with a flame emoji and a hotdog. I stifle a snort, and my gaze darts to Aiden. Jeez, I can feel the heat in my cheeks. He smiles back, then hits the close button.

He can't see the screen. He can't see the screen. I repeat this to myself as I grip my phone, feeling as if my embarrassment is another entity in the elevator, impossible for him to miss. I scoot to the back of the elevator and type out:

> Effigy successfully burned

The doors open on the lobby, and we follow the family out and turn left for the continental breakfast area. I put my phone away. It beeps again with another text, but I ignore it. Whatever Claire's sent can wait a sec. Aiden and I split up to peruse our choices. I snag a bowl of oatmeal and layer brown sugar and pecans and raisins on that sucker. Compensating? Maybe. It's *my* oatmeal. I also grab a banana, along with OJ and hot tea, and head over to a two-top.

Aiden's still piling his plate high, so I pull out my phone.

> Good job. I'll call you
> tonight to hear how your
> day went. OK?

I tap out an agreement. Aiden plops down two plates filled with bacon, eggs, a waffle, and Lord knows what else. A few pieces of fruit stand bravely, surrounded by the sea of protein and gluten. He swings his leg over the back of the chair and sits. I shouldn't find it sexy, but I do.

After he downs an impressive amount of food, he looks up. The sunlight streaming through the window hits him at such an angle the faint, pale hairs on his cheeks are visible, which then changes to darker stubble—almost reddish—along his jaw.

The sunlight's also doing its thing to his light-brown eyes, making them lighter, and I can make out flecks of gold.

"So...a castle, huh?" he asks, pulling me out of my embarrassing frolic across the features of his face.

Screw it. Full-on dork it is. He sees me as a weirdo, book nerd, right? So why not confess.

He'll be turned off even more, and that'd be a good thing.

"Yeah, this trip is to help me find myself." Who knows, maybe talking freely will prove to myself that we're just friends and only friends.

"You're lost?"

"Ha. Funny." I put down my mug of tea. "No. You know Claire, from the women's team? She feels like I need to"—I hold up my fingers and make air quotes—"get out of my shell, and she's the organizer and instigator of this trip. Complete with all the stops and the timeline. I'm supposed to journal it and live in the moment, that kind of crap."

I expect him to crack a joke. Heck, three sentences back I expected him to lose eye focus. Instead, he's listened solemnly to the whole recital. Of course, I leave out that he's one of the main reasons for Claire goading me into this.

He leans back, both eyebrows up. "So the first stop's Solomon's Castle. What'll we find there?"

I fiddle with my unused knife, twirling it back and forth, back and forth, on the smooth table top. "Honestly? I don't know. I meant to Google it when I got into the room last night and then I, er, forgot."

More like I was hand-flapping flustered about having him right next door, agonizing whether to play it cool and invite him over to watch a movie or play cards or...something. Then I marched around the room chanting, "Stupid-stupidstupid." Then I chastised myself for even engaging in all these mental gymnastics. Especially because he was probably conked out already with nary a thought about me on the other side of a *door*.

I look up.

"So we'll both be surprised." He gives a wide grin and eats a whole piece of bacon.

"Yeah."

My decision to not care what I say or do feels like the right one—because he's not worth the mental energy—but I'm feeling strangely vulnerable. As if I'm here, with him, without any shield, and he's calmly sitting there, listening, accepting.

To keep going with the we're-just-friends convo, I ask, "You guys ready for your game? It's the playoffs, right?" Hopefully, this'll push his intense focus off me.

"Yep." He wipes his mouth with a napkin. "Southeast Division. Whoever wins goes to the national championships in Chicago. It'll be tough competition, but we have an advantage—it's such a new sport, everyone playing is on the same skill level."

"So you stand a good chance?"

He props his elbows on the table and leans in. "That's what we're hoping."

Just that little movement puts him closer in my space, and my stomach gets all swoopy again, especially because I can now catch a whiff of his masculine scent. By now, he's inhaled everything on his two plates, and I'm looking at his flat stomach hidden by his gray T-shirt and wondering where the heck he puts it all. But I guess that's what a lot of exercise does for ya.

How am I going to resist him?

Aiden

At breakfast, I was going to ask Jane about bailing, honest, but first I was on a mission to fill my belly, and then I was enjoying our casual, easygoing conversation. Like the night we met, we clicked, conversation flowed, and I wasn't using most of my energy to charm and deflect.

And fuck me, but I didn't want to jinx our reacquired ease. Not again anyway. Several weeks ago at her place, I'd woken up, and there was an awkwardness usually only experienced when I sleep with a woman. A situation I know how to handle. Usually by being crystal clear from the get-go what we both want out of our night together.

Except, this time, while we did *sleep* together, it was only in the literal sense. No sex.

So why the awkwardness?

Who knows, but that night I took leave of my senses, and I don't know if I'll ever get them back.

Now I'm up in my room, stuffing the few things I'd taken out of my bag back into it. Jane had some things to do downstairs before we left, and I'm to meet her where we had breakfast. I didn't argue. It's her trip. I throw a dollar on the bureau for the maid, sling the duffel bag onto my shoulder, and march to the door. I grip the handle.

Fuck it—I decided my plan last night, didn't I? When we get to the car, I'll ask Jane to drop me off at the MegaBus stop in Tampa after the castle thing.

I push out the door and head to the elevator bank. Oddly, that decision doesn't sit as well as I thought it would.

I use the alone time to check in with Stuart. "How'd it go last night?" I ask as soon as he answers. "Did the fan hold up?" I hit the down button.

"Like a champ. Good receipts too."

"Good to hear. Call me if anything comes up, okay?"

"Will do."

I'm about to hang up when he says, "Hey, did you collect

a bar tab before you left?"

"No. Why?"

"Cuz we were sixty-five dollars over in cash."

I pause on my way into the elevator. Well, that's a pleasant change. Normally, my managers pocket the overage, because, you know, it costs me squat to operate the damn place and keep them employed.

"Check with Mandy. I saw her with one of the regulars."

"Will do. We've got this. Enjoy your vacation, boss."

"Thanks." I hang up and stare at my cell.

Huh. Looks as if I found my dream bar manager.

Soon enough, I'm downstairs, and I find Jane in the dining area, sitting at the same table, her suitcase alongside. On the table is her journal, and she's staring at it, tapping a green pen against the table, mouth pursed.

A new Polaroid's pasted in, of the breakfast area, but nothing's written next to it.

"Ready?" I ask.

"Yep. Let's go." She tosses her pens into her messenger bag and grabs her journal and suitcase handle.

We stroll down the hall and out to the car in companionable silence. But as the daylight bathes us, and her warm presence fills the space beside me, I'm reluctant to ask about dropping me off in Tampa. Somehow, today feels different than last night's sleep-deprived panic.

We toss our bags into her trunk and slip inside her car, already warm from the morning sun.

She tucks her journal into the space between the seats, puts her cell into its dash-holder, and plugs in the address for Solomon's Castle. "Lots of small roads, but according to Google, we'll be there in twenty-five minutes." She slides her key into the ignition. "It opens at eleven, so that'll be perfect."

She turns the key, and there's a clicking noise. "Weird." She tries again. On the third turn, it starts.

"Does that happen a lot?"

Frowning, she shifts the car into reverse and scans the rearview mirror. "No. This car's normally pretty reliable."

"When's the last time you replaced the battery?"

"Last year, so it should be good."

Her car's one of those dependable foreign models, but still I can't help but worry. Maybe it was just a fluke. But now I can't seem to open my mouth and ask about Tampa.

Which is okay. We still have to go to this castle first, *then* head north. I'll ask her then.

6

Jane

We're in the middle of friggin' nowhere.

Thank God for GPS. The Google gods guide me through a series of turns along back roads lined on either side with swaths of flat cow-land, punctuated here and there with stubby bushes, and an occasional lone, scraggly tree.

Earlier this morning, as I pasted in the requisite snapshot of where I stayed, I studied The Rules and found my loophole.

Oh, Claire planned this trip well. But not well enough. I did some quick math with the miles between each designated nightly stop and smiled.

By limiting my distance covered each day, she meant to force me to slow down and not zip through each stop.

Fine.

But I don't have to spend that time *at the sites*. No lie, I did hop in my seat when I realized I can still zip through the sites, take a snapshot or two, write a few lines, then, *fist pump*, check in early at the hotel and still have my ideal vacation—curling up and *reading.*

I glance at Aiden, who's flipping through my phone's playlist.

The side bennie to my plan?

Less time with him.

Feeling comfortable for the first time since Claire handed me the gift-wrapped box, I relax and tap my fingers to the tune he's queued up.

Perfect. This will work out perfect. And I have a TBR pile of biblical proportions on my tablet.

Not getting all worked up about what Aiden thinks of me was the right call. Because as the scenery cruises by and one tune spills into another, I'm not at all caring if we talk or not.

Aiden's an easygoing guy. I'll give him that.

It's too bad he's a playboy.

Abruptly, the scenery switches to a dense wall of palmetto, more scraggly bushes, and old oaks dripping with Spanish moss. A hand-painted sign saying "Solomon's Castle" in red block letters with an arrow pointing right appears.

"You have arrived at your destination," announces Google maps.

Farther ahead, I pull into a marked-off parking area. All right. Let's get this over with.

My hand's on the door handle, but his voice stops me. "Hold up."

I glance over, and I swear to all the swoony alpha heroes in the romances I've read that his eyes have that certain sparkle.

Huh. Thought that was only in books.

I raise a brow. I'm immune. I *am*.

"You still in the dark on what this place is?"

"Yep." I figure I'll find out soon enough. "You?"

"Yep," he says cheerily. "Let's guess."

I roll my eyes, grab my journal and purse, and open the door. I want him to say—no, actually I *expect* him to say—*you're no fun.*

I'm ready for it, because I want to say, so badly, *good.*

But he doesn't. He jumps out and says, "Obviously, it's gonna be a castle. Or is it? Maybe it's supposed to be ironic, and it's a grotto, and everyone knows it but wants to see *why* he thinks it's a castle. Or maybe it's castle-y in its grottoness."

Despite myself, I huff a breath of laughter. "A grotto? In the middle of Florida swampland?"

"Okay, so not a grotto." He shuts his door. "Maybe it's a Swiss Family Robinson thing he's got going on, with cypress trees and shit. That'd be cool."

"It'll be a castle," I say.

In front of us, a decorative white metal gate stands open. Across the top of one gate is the word "Solomon's" crafted in metal with a medieval-y font. The silhouette of a woman takes up part of the gate. The other gate's similar but with a knight and the word "Castle."

Aiden jumps in front of the knight-half of the gate. "Take my pic."

Reluctantly, I pull out the Polaroid. He strikes a super-serious pose, one arm across his middle, the other arm's elbow propped on his forearm. He grips his chin in a Thinking Man pose. I expect an eyebrow to cock, but instead both go up as if he's surprised.

I smile, line up the shot, then catch the film when it ejects on the other side.

"Cool." He grabs the almost-square, thick, plastic-y paper and shakes it.

"That doesn't actually speed things along, you know."

"Yep. But it's fun to think it does," he says and winks. He nods to another couple walking by us.

Before I realize what I'm doing, I'm beside him, watching the blank, gray surface turn milky and slowly resolve into full color.

Mistake. I accidentally get a whiff of his masculine scent warmed by the Florida sunshine, and all along my skin, prickles pop up and dance.

I swear to God, my body gets all irrational when in his vicinity. As if there's an invisible force that works on me when I get in range.

But I ignore it, because what good does it do me? It's not as if it matters. I'd be one more conquest. That is, if he even wanted me. Which clearly, he doesn't.

I focus on the snapshot. It's a dorky shot, but dangit, it's cute.

His chuckle is low, and the deep tones sizzle all across my stupid skin—you know, the one that's prickling already from his nearness. He hands it to me. "Let's see this swamp castle."

I stick the photo into the back of the journal and follow him along the path.

And then we stop as the building comes into view.

"Not a grotto," he says.

"It *is* a castle," I say.

"Huh," he grunts.

We stand there because, yeah, in front of us *is* a two-story castle complete with turrets and stained-glass windows.

But. Made of shiny reflective metal, like tinfoil. Not stone.

Aiden rubs his hands together. "*This* has a story behind it." He glances back at me, grins, and marches down the path.

Before I realize it, I've pulled out the Polaroid. Careful to frame it so Aiden looks like one of the other visitors milling out front, I take a picture.

I rush to catch up, but he stops by a life-sized white plaster horse on the side lawn. "Real brick, or just painted?" He points to its hooves.

"Odd." I stick the new Polaroid in the back of the journal and move closer. "And what a strange expression on his face." His tongue—or is it his lower lip?—is protruding, giving him a dopey look. "He looks like a horse Don Quixote would ride."

Aiden holds his hand out and makes a give-it-here gesture at the camera. Folks don't react to my literary references, so Aiden blipping right past it does *not* wound. It doesn't. Some think I do it to be snobby, but they're wrong. These things just pop out, and I regret it instantly.

If this had been a real date with a guy I was interested in, I'd be kicking myself right now.

Instead, I give an internal shrug and hand him the Polaroid. He waves me over to stand by the horse.

I get up right next to it, and Aiden steps back to get

me in range. "Say cheese," he says, his mouth just visible below the camera.

Right before he snaps the pic, something bubbles up inside me and makes me stick out my tongue in imitation of the horse.

"Nice," he deadpans.

The distinct noise of a Polaroid follows, and the film shoots out.

Again, I'm next to him, waiting, before I realize what I've done. It's a good excuse, right? I'm only standing here to see the film develop, that's all. I'm loving this excuse.

When my goofy face swims into view next to the white horse, Aiden says, "Poor Rocinante. Forever tilting at windmills."

I swear to God, I hear the ole-timey record scratch in my mind. I'm standing here stock still while inside I'm going wait-wait-rewind-rewind, complete with expansive arm movements, that he just referenced the dang *horse* from *Don Quixote*, and he just gives the snapshot a flick.

"That's a keeper." He hands it to me, and I mutely stash it into my journal.

Then, for my own self-preservation, I shove that literary nugget into a corner of my mind and bury it in a bunch of nope-nope-nope. For him to be hot as heck *and* well-read?

No. Just no.

Jane

AIDEN MAKES A slow circuit of the castle's foyer, both eyebrows raised. "Again. Not what I expected."

No kidding.

After we pay our entrance fee, a tour guide gathers us

around. Metal sculptures pack the lobby, and folk art crowds the walls, all made with what look like found objects.

We follow the sonorous sing-song voice of the tour guide, who tells us the owner, Howard Solomon, was the artist for all of this, plus the architect and builder of the structure itself. Each object is described in reverent, memorized lines, highlighting the creator's goofy, on-the-nose humor.

Aiden sticks by my side as we work our way through the various rooms. At one point, he starts playing with his phone. Well, that didn't take long.

No sympathy from me. I lift my chin and return my attention to the tour guide. I'd warned him this trip could be boring.

Okay, yeah, I thought it would be too. But surprisingly, I'm not seeing this as interfering with my chance to get back to reading about Daphne and Rupert's sizzling dialogue and adventures in Egypt.

Aiden says in an undertone, "They call him the Da Vinci of Debris."

"What?"

He holds up his phone. "Just looked him up." He pockets it and once again listens to the guide.

We tour the whole downstairs and also the upstairs, which contains Solomon's living quarters. It's a lot to take in.

One thing I know, Solomon was never bored a day in his long life.

Back outside by the green benches, Aiden gazes up at the silver structure. He points. "*That* is a castle."

And I know what he means. Solomon wanted to create a home, to his own vision, and he did. He didn't care what anyone would think, or how weird they might think him.

"My grandmother would love this place," I say.

"Yeah?"

I nod. "She loves carving creatures with wood she finds and using scavenged objects to stick on them to create their clothes or hats or what-have-you. After Hurricane Charley blew through, she made a troll with some of the downed tree limbs, complete with a mini saw and Spanish moss for hair."

"So your typical grandma, then."

I laugh. "Yeah, that, she is not." I point to the left. "Hungry?"

"Heck yeah."

What I'm pointing at? The restaurant? It's a Spanish Galleon. Because of course it is. Its wooden sides are visible through the break in the trees. There's also a gift shop inside. We order sandwiches and exit out the far side. A wide-open patio with tables and chairs beckons under the canopy of trees.

A breeze brushes our skin, welcome in the July heat, and we pick a table in the shade.

I set my tray down, he sets his down, and, boom, I'm back in my shell as I sit across from him, because this feels too much like a date.

It's not a date, I tell myself.

It's not.

7

Aiden

I'm sprawled on a green bench waiting for Jane, my arms stretched along the seat back, soaking in the unusually balmy weather. By far, this is one of the kookiest spots I've ever seen. I love it.

And though she won't admit it—yet—I know Jane enjoyed herself too.

We were also back to our easygoing interaction from the night we met. Until we sat down for lunch.

Still puzzling that shift.

I stand. *What the—?*

Why am I even wondering? Wondering about how we're *interacting?* She's a long-term kind of girl. And that's not my type.

So…we're good. Yep. I blow out a breath of relief. The only thing I should worry about is leaving her alone with that car. All during the drive here it worried me, especially seeing how isolated this area is.

She appears through the break in the trees, the weathered wooden sides of the Boat-in-the-Moat restaurant behind her. And she's sporting the biggest grin.

Shit.

That grin is doing some voodoo in my gut. Yeah, this

trip is looking more and more like one of my more epic mistakes. Instead of shedding her from my system by being on a *boring* road trip with her, she's only verifying my initial impression of her.

Maybe I'm coming down with something. Tampa. I can get off in Tampa. If her car starts, I'll ask.

When she nears, she thumbs behind her. "There's a sign above the bathroom doors that says, 'Rooms To Go.'"

"Forget Da Vinci of Debris, that guy was the King of Corny Jokes."

"Right? The whole time during the tour I kept wanting to go—"

She mimes hitting a drum kit, and I provide the sound effects. "Ba-dum-tissshhh."

She's still got that grin on her face, and it's definitely the grin affecting me, not a cold. It's as if I'm seeing all of her, unfettered. I fall in step with her as we head back to the car. I pass her a small paper bag. "Got ya something."

She opens the bag and pulls out the postcard I bought at the gift shop.

"For your journal," I say, since she seems lost on why she needs a postcard.

"Thank you." And just like that, she appears to curl into herself again.

Weird.

But she sticks it into the back of her journal. And as we walk side by side to the parking lot, a heavy weight descends on me. I finally identify the feeling: dread. The cause? That her car will start fine. That I'll leave her alone and *then* the car breaks down. That I'll leave and…miss her.

I pull in a deep breath. "So where next, Don Quixote?" Decision made, something shifts inside that makes things feel *right*.

"Up north to Lake Wales, to something called Spook Hill, and then on to…" Here she turns her head away, and I can't hear the rest.

"To where?"

She walks around to the driver's side of the car and arches that little dark brow. "To the Potty Chair."

Breath explodes from me. "A *potty* chair? What's weird about a potty chair, except for someone thinking it'd make a great tourist spot?" We've only been to one spot, yeah, but this is *Claire* who devised this trip. The theme's clear: weird.

"It's twenty-four feet tall," she says with no inflection.

After dropping that nugget, she steps into her car. We parked in the shade, so the inside's not as hot as it could be, but thankfully, she starts the car and cranks the A/C.

"Okay. That *is* weird," I concede as relief floods me that I decided to continue on this crazy trip whether her car started or not.

We move to buckle up, and our hands brush. We both tense. Me, because for some reason, a jolt of—okay. Fuck this. It wasn't a jolt of desire. No way. It was…surprise.

That's all it was.

She tensed, because…memory of our sexually charged standoff outside her door last night comes crashing back.

From the corner of my eye, I see she's looking at me too. A softness in her eyes scrambles my brain. Her gaze drops to my lips, and, Jesus fuck, mine drops to hers. Again admiring the asymmetry.

It's as if she's rocking a lip mullet, but, you know, sexy. Unlike a mullet. Business up top, with its conservative lines, and party on the bottom, with its plump, kissable…

I pull away on a sharp inhale as I realize we'd both drifted a shade closer.

That was close. Too close. *Get your head screwed on right, Aiden.* I fiddle with the air vents, getting the ones on my side angled just right. Yeah, a little more to the right. And up. There we go. Perfect. Yep.

"I've got a new rule," I say, trying to make my voice all normal.

She clears her throat and clamps her cell into her dashboard holster. "What's that?" Her voice is slightly higher-pitched than usual.

"Claire wants to encourage you to be spontaneous, right?"

"Maybe."

"There's no *maybe*." I risk eye contact now that I'm back in control of myself. "Part of what made this visit so awesome was because we neglected to Google it. We had no idea what to expect. Normally, we don't have that luxury."

She looks away briefly from typing in the next destination address into her cell and pins me with her serious gaze. "What do you mean?"

"If you or I were planning this trip, we'd have done the research and picked these spots, and so we'd already know what we are in for."

She nods and resumes typing into her cell.

I prop my arm on the seat and turn to her. "My new proposed rule is that we don't look up info, other than directions, for each site."

Her bottom lip moves across her top one, as if she's tasting the option. My dick chubs up a little at the sight.

"Do I have a second?"

She smiles. "Second."

I sit forward and stretch out my legs. "So moved."

"You're ridiculous."

"Yeah, but you love it." Then I realize what I said, and I cover it by giving a mock innocent whistle and looking out the front window.

"Aiden?"

I look back at her. "Yes?"

She looks a bit shy, and I'm worried what the hell she's going to risk saying. "Thanks for the postcard."

Um… I give a confused shake of my head. "You're welcome." I rub my hands together. "So what's your guess on what Spook Hill is?"

Jane

About an hour and a half later, we cruise into the town of Lake Wales. From the map, we're even more in the center of the state, almost due south of Orlando, and straight east of Tampa.

Aiden's made a game of figuring out our future stops, and we've ranked our guesses.

Spook Hill could be:

5. Where a famous person was murdered and his ghost comes out at night.

That was my one of my guesses, but it's ranked number five, because Aiden argued that if true, then Claire would have stipulated visiting at night. I conceded the point.

4. A cemetery perpetually covered in mist.

That one was Aiden's, and I pointed out that mist would gather in lower areas, not higher ones, so unless Spook Hill's not really a hill... He conceded the point. Which leaves us with our top three.

3. A low-budget horror house, with some side guesses on cost of admission.

2. A Florida rip-off of Boot Hill.

1. A misunderstood faerie ring.

We turn onto the street for Spook Hill, and the neighborhood's a mixture of empty fields and older, ranch-style homes. Up ahead, a black and white sign greets us with the words "Legend of Spook Hill" and a drawing of a Casper-like ghost.

"Ooh, a legend," Aiden says with relish.

I pull onto the shoulder, and we get out to read the sign.

When we finish, Aiden says, "The ghost of an alligator and a Native American chief who killed each other in a battle? Clearly we're forgetting to take into account the Florida wacky factor with our guesses."

I glance up the road and find the white line bisecting the black asphalt. Our starting point. I shake my head. "I'll believe it when I see it. There's no way we'll coast uphill." Apparently the site is some kind of gravity-defying spot, controlled by the ghost of the alligator or the chief. The sign's not too clear on that point.

Aiden butts his shoulder into mine. "Aw, c'mon. Let's try it."

"Oh, we'll try it, but it's not physically possible." I hand him my Polaroid and stand in front of the sign for my requisite journal shot. He snaps a pic, then stands next to me, holds his arm out, and hits the button again.

The one of me is like I expect. It gets the job done for Claire—shows me here where she wanted me. The second one…it slowly resolves, and we snort at the same time. It's just our foreheads at the very bottom of the frame with both of his eyebrows raised and only one of mine.

I stick them into my journal with the other ones and his postcard, and we scramble back into the car.

As directed by the sign, I drive up to the white line that bisects the road. We're at the slight well between two inclines. "Okay, Spook Hill, let's see what you've got." I shift into neutral and wait.

At first nothing happens. Since we're on a public street, I keep an eye on the rearview mirror for other cars. Then the car starts rolling backward.

"Holy shit," Aiden says.

"What? We're on a slight incline, so of course we're going to have a little momentum." Lame.

"No. We're going uphill."

"No, we aren't."

We debate what's going on, and since no other cars are around, I park and get out. I point to the white line and where it is on the road. "See. We started out slightly uphill."

"I don't think that can account for all of it. We were going faster than I'd expect."

Is he nuts? "We were barely moving."

He looks at me like *I'm* nuts, so I say, "Let's do it again."

We hop back in and pull up to the white line. And again

we slowly roll down and up.

But Aiden points ahead, even though that's not the direction we're going in. "See, we're moving faster than you'd think."

"I can't look forward. I've got to keep an eye in back." But the oddity of him pointing forward while we're creeping back has me wondering. "Let's switch. You drive and look back."

We do it again, and this time I look forward. "Whoa," I say, at the same time he says, "Huh, it's not working."

I look at his puzzled face and smile. "It's an optical illusion. You have to be facing forward to get the full effect."

"Well, I'll be damned."

And then he gives me a big grin that lights up his whole face. "Well played, Spook Hill. Well played."

I laugh. "Indeed."

"So. Potty Chair?"

"Potty Chair."

And for the first time since this trip started, I'm looking forward to the next stop.

8

Jane

My anticipation lasts as long as ten minutes, when, in Florida fashion, the sunny weather flips and it's raining in sheets.

We'd hoped to move away from it, or that it'd end soon, but as we turn onto the street for the giant potty, the rain's coming down in a steady beat.

As best we can tell, we're in a section of Winter Haven that's part rural, part suburban, with matching one-story ranches plopped onto large tracts, interspersed here and there with a McMansion.

I peer out the window on his side, which is supposedly where this structure will appear. "Not where I'd expect an oversized potty chair."

"Nobody expects an oversized potty chair," he says, imitating the cadence and accent of the Spanish Inquisition line from a Monty Python skit.

I chuckle, but then I'm reminded of our fun movie night, when we burrowed under blankets and hung out as if we were two people who'd been best friends for a long time instead of just meeting that night.

It was exactly like the meet-cutes you read about in romances, and I'd been fooled. Sucked in. Saw the whole night and everything we said or did through some kind of this-is-significant lens. Yeah, I started out thinking this was a chance to see what the whole casual sex fuss was about. But that didn't last long. Nope. Because I discovered he was a cool, fun guy that I really clicked with, I interpreted our night together as sweet. The start of a nice, slow get-to-know-you.

But when I found out the next morning from Claire that he was a love-em-and-leave-em playboy? It put a completely different spin on the night: we hadn't hooked up because he had no interest in me at all.

It was a sobering realization.

I know I'm insecure, and that it's not an attractive quality, but I'm not some heroine in a romance novel who needs to be strong and inspiring, so deal. I'm just me.

"There it is." Aiden points.

I pull over into the grass. Sure enough, a giant white chair squats in this guy's lawn. From here, it's hard to see what makes it a potty chair.

"Okay. Take the Polaroid. I'm going to run out so you can snap a pic with it in the background. Then we'll keep going."

He sits straighter. "What? No way."

I pause with my elbow against the seat, leaning into the back looking for the camera. I look up at him. "You won't get wet. Just roll down the window."

He rolls his eyes and turns into the seat so he's sitting sideways. "I could give a flying fuck about getting wet. No. We're both going to go all the way over to that chair and *see* it."

I stare at him. "It's raining."

"It's not lightning." He puts a hand on the door handle. "Come on, it'll be fun."

I can tell he won't let up. The quicker we get out there, the quicker we can be back. "I still need a pic, though, and we can't get the Polaroid wet."

"Okay." He leans past me and grabs the camera from the back seat, which brings him—his heat, his scent—right into my space. "We'll nab a shot first. Then I'll join you out there."

I snatch my umbrella, clamber out, and scoot around to his side of the car. With the potty chair lined up behind me, I face him, spread one arm out wide, and stick out my tongue.

The rain beats down on my umbrella and my exposed forearm as I wait. When the film ejects, I spin around and start walking to the potty chair.

The car door opens and closes.

Wait. He doesn't have an umbrella. I start to turn around, feeling a little ashamed it took me that long to realize.

Just as I complete my about-face, a blur fills my vision and a strong arm clamps around my waist, pulling me up against a wet torso. I give a little squeak.

"Wicked woman," Aiden says by my ear. "You were going to let me get wet."

"I was just coming back for you!"

"Uh-huh. Sure."

"I swear. See, I'm facing this way." But then I search his face, and while he's not smiling and has a serious look about him, his eyes are again doing that stupid, twinkling thing.

He's having to stoop to fit under the umbrella, so I raise it higher. The rain's beating all around us in this grassy field, there's a twenty-four foot potty chair behind us, but for some reason I'm standing here, looking up at him, and all I want to do is kiss him like *whoa*.

For a second, I indulge the fantasy. Pretend this hot man could actually be attracted to me.

When we'd gotten back in the car at the castle, there was a moment when I thought, *holy cow, he's going to kiss me*. But then he pulled away.

I need to stop reading romance novels.

I'm not his type. I'm a book nerd. He's a jock who owns a bar, for Pete's sake.

He clears his throat and looks over my shoulder. "C'mon, let's check it out."

Right. Because that's what we're doing. He wasn't about to kiss me.

Despite that potent reminder, I'm tingling all over. Must

be an aftershock. As if just the possibility of a kiss under an umbrella in the rain was enough to reverberate through me.

Jeez, I need to get out more.

Even though we have an umbrella keeping us dry, we hobble-run for the shelter of the potty chair, our gaits erratic as we attempt to keep pace, stay under the umbrella, and not bump each other out of the way.

Under the giant chair, I lower the umbrella and shake it.

I look up. Because Aiden's strangely quiet.

Yep, there's a hole. It's a twenty-four-foot-tall white chair with a hole in the seat.

"Hey, there's writing," Aiden says.

I squint past the late afternoon sun peeping through the rain clouds. Sure enough, printed on the underside, there are the words "Put Your Trust Here," followed by a set of coordinates and then "Put Your Trust There" and another set of coordinates.

Aiden pulls out his phone. "Time for Google." He taps away.

"True. It's not cheating since we're already here."

He looks down at me with an amused expression. "Nope. It's not cheating." He peers back up. "I wish we could climb to the top."

"Are you serious?"

"Of course. Especially because according to this"—he holds up his phone—"if we were up on the seat, we'd be looking through the, er, hole at this." He waves to the ceiling directly overhead. "And on *that* side, there's a giant clown face."

"Get out."

He moves closer and holds out his phone.

I lean closer. Wow, yeah, there's a giant clown, with his mouth where the hole is. "This is so weird."

"Gets weirder. Check it out." He scrolls the website up. "The artist calls it a HOHO chair, and it's supposed to represent a wormhole portal to a Marcel Duchamp art installation at the Philadelphia Museum of Art."

I look back up at the underside. "Which is the second set of coordinates, I'm guessing."

"Yep. He even has a video that's supposed to simulate what happens if you drop something through the hole."

We watch this mad scientist kind of video, complete with whirling colored swirls for the wormhole. While it's pretty apparent, even at the start, that the video isn't going to get much more interesting, I'm watching avidly, because, okay, it's nice standing right next to Aiden. He's warm, dangit. Standing close like this helps me pretend for a little while longer.

"Well," I say when the video ends, my gaze still fixed on his phone.

"Yep," he says. He pulls up another article on the HOHO chair.

"Humans are weird."

He gives a low rumble of a chuckle, and because I'm so close, I can feel it transmit physically, from his body to mine.

Now the tingling along my skin starts to bunch around my lady parts.

Huh.

Never had *that* happen.

He pockets his phone and turns so he's facing me but still just as close. I have to arch my neck to see his face.

I catch my breath—there's a big grin there, beaming all of its hunky, charming glory right at me. How's a lady supposed to resist?

His blond hair, darkened from the rain, is plastered to his forehead, with a little curl flirting with his right cheekbone. I flex my fingers because—gah—I really really want to reach up and slick his hair back for him. I glance at his mouth again.

The scene from the 2005 version of *Pride and Prejudice* pops into my head, the one where Mr. Darcy is all yummy and wet, and he's laying his heart out right there for Lizzy, and she's all, "I wouldn't marry you if you're the last man on earth," and he looks so devastated but also as if he's dying to kiss her.

Except this man's not proposing, and I'm under a giant potty chair and not in some garden temple thing.

Except, holy mackerel. He's leaning down.

His strong hand cups my cheek. I hold my breath, my heart going omg-omg-omg.

Next thing I know, I'm clutching his wet T-shirt and yanking him down. I think because I was afraid it wasn't actually happening and I didn't want to be disappointed again?

Who knows, but our mouths bump into each other.

Smooth, Jane.

Just as mortification is about to yank me back to sanity, he groans and brushes his lips across mine. His face is warm but wet from the rain. He shifts his hand to the back of my neck and grips me tighter.

Holy heck. We're kissing. His tongue makes a foray, and I welcome him, his mouth a warm contrast to his rain-wet skin.

And then something amazing happens—a warmth bursts in my chest and arrows down. I've kissed guys before, but I've never, ever, been turned on by a lip-lock. Not like this.

It's always been just fun…or interesting.

But this? Sparks are a-sizzling, baby, all along my skin.

I angle closer, and his other hand grasps my hip and tugs me up against him. Oh jeez—my heart thumps—because there's no mistaking the hard-on pushing into my lower belly.

He does a slow circle of his hips, groans, and breaks away.

My breaths are coming fast, so I breathe through my nose, trying to disguise how I embarrassingly sound as if I just ran ten laps.

"Jane?"

"Yes?"

"You realize what we were doing, right?"

"Um, kissing?" I'm still trying to get my breathing disguised and under control, so I can't spare a lot for thinking.

"Yes. Under. A. Potty. Chair."

We start laughing, and then our laughter feeds off each other as we trail off, and then start laughing again. It's one of those good kinds of belly laughs, when your stomach feels as if it did a bunch of crunches.

"One for the books." Aaaand… I release my death grip on his T-shirt because, like a dope, I was still holding on.

"I'll say." He gives me a sly wink.

I flush, because I'm like eighty-percent positive there's a double meaning to that. Or maybe it's just my imagination again.

I pick my umbrella up from where I'd dropped it. "Well, we better get going if we're going to make it to Daytona Beach tonight."

His eyebrows shoot up. "Daytona Beach?"

"Yep." I step out from under the potty chair and hold the umbrella high so he can squeeze in under, and we walk back to the car.

"Do I even want to ask?" His fist is gripping the umbrella, stacked above mine. We keep our strides in sync, him all casual, and me like ohmygodwejustkissed.

I match my tone to his lighthearted one. "The next site is actually a hotel. The Sun Viking Lodge. Claire booked a room."

And then I stumble, breaking our in-sync stride—Claire only booked one room. Surely there'll be more available.

Aiden must think the ground made me stumble, because he turns into my side, placing his hand across my stomach as if he's saving me from a face-plant. "You okay?"

I nod mutely because his thumb just did a little circle. God, that feels nice.

He moves back to the less mind-altering position of being by my side. "Sun Viking Lodge. Lemme guess—it'll have Vikings."

And because I don't want to show I'm anxious about tonight, I play along. "Vikings in the *sun*."

Yeah, there'll be rooms.

9

Aiden

"No rooms." I blow out a breath and put my cell down. I scoured various travel sites trying to book a room for myself, and now we just passed Orlando.

The first place I tried, of course, was the Sun Viking Lodge, but they were booked. So then I tried hotels in ever increasing distances from there. No luck.

"How can that be?"

"Some gymnastics convention-competition thing with kids and families from all over the country." I finally called the Viking Lodge in desperation to see if they knew of anything remotely nearby that might not be on the travel sites. The guy was understanding, told me the scoop, and that everything was booked.

I'm trying extra hard, because she's getting more and more nervous about this situation. I can sympathize.

Holy hell.

That kiss.

I think it goes without saying that that kiss was unplanned. It's just that…when she glanced at my mouth, for perhaps the third time today, the tension that's been thrumming through me ever since we started this trip had me wanting to see—is there more here?

Her yanking me to her cleared that up.

I shift in my seat, but the damn woody I've been sporting since The Potty Chair Kiss will not go away.

She also went quiet following my bad news. She has different levels of quietness. One level, she's right there with me in the moment and we're enjoying each other's company with no pressure to *perform* with jokes or conversation.

But then there's another level, where she draws in on herself, and there's a weight in the air surrounding her, shielding her, distancing her from everyone else.

This quiet now is a new level. There's a trace of nervousness and vulnerability, as if she's almost at the surface, but unsure if she can make an appearance.

I look out the windshield and don't say anything. I'm tempted to coax her, but I have a hunch she needs to break through on her own, like those nature documentaries that show hatching babies and how they have to push through the shell on their own to gain the necessary strength to survive outside it.

Plus, there's the not-so-small matter of her ghosting me.

She unclamps her fingers from the steering wheel and rubs her palms back and forth on the wheel. She grips it again. "Um, we can…can see if my room has a double, and we can share it. I won't mind, if you don't."

Obviously that took a lot for her to say, so I don't draw attention to it. No jokes. No innuendo. No teasing. Instead, I say, "Thank you. If not, rooms usually have a club chair I can crash in." I fiddle with the air vent.

"Maybe they'll have a roll-away bed we can have them bring up." Her voice is a tad higher with false optimism.

"Sure. It'll all work out. I know you didn't plan for me to be along."

She rubs her palms on the wheel again. "I'm glad you're along." She pushes the words out in a rush as if shoving them with a temporary courage that could disappear any moment.

I glance at her, and her cheeks are blushing. "Yeah?"

"Yeah."

Inexplicably, my whole chest gets warm. I nod and smile. I'll do whatever will make her comfortable tonight, but a growing part of me—like, literally—hopes she'll allow me to sleep in *her* bed.

I adjust my ass in the seat and stretch out my legs, giving a discreet tug to my jeans. Tonight's potential pulses in the close confines of the car and feeds on the simmering pull that's been a constant. I'm hyper aware of where she is and how close. Where her hands are. When they move and where. And it's driving me batshit because none of the positions are where I want them to be—in my hand.

Fuck, that's sappy.

But dammit, it's true.

And that truth hits me like the strongest shot of whiskey— the jolt of surprise, the heat, the thrill.

We've got wicked chemistry, and sure, I've been an idiot thinking it would wane with road-trip familiarity. Instead, this trip has solidified my initial assessment—she's awesome. Someone I enjoy being around. My words aren't the stuff of poetry—I can't explain it any better than we just *fit*. And it feels as if we've always known each other.

Another mile marker speeds by as I soak in this truth. And like a shot of whiskey, there's the inevitable sobering moment—I'm good for hookups. I'm not relationship material.

Tuesday night, when Luke accused me of being a manwhore and said that I need to stop, I dismissed his advice. My meaningless hookups not only numbed me but also kept me from getting sucked into another long-term relationship.

Now I'm staring down the last years of my twenties, and the whole hookup thing just leaves me feeling like a shallow jackass. It's done fuck-all for me. Except maybe help numb my pain so I could ferry myself from the Brittany-shore to… wherever I am now.

But… I'm here on this new shore, and that pain now seems so distant.

I glance at Jane, and again warmth fills my chest. Maybe it's time I let go of that crutch.

Jane

Holy heck.

That kiss.

And now we're going to share a *room*? I flush again for like the umpteenth time, the heat going into every nook and cranny of my body. It's like I'm some blinking light, blushing over and over, since our kiss under the potty chair. I'm not fooling myself that this situation is anything more than what it is. He's a player—I know that. And we've been in close proximity for over twenty-four hours, so of course he'd make a move on me since there's no one else around. It's not *me* me that he's interested in—I'm just a warm body.

Warm body... Aiden's warm body.

Another mile marker whizzes by as I, dangit, flush again, and my mind does a little side trip into fantasy land, picturing how, in an alternate world, he *doesn't* sleep in the club chair and instead climbs into bed with *me*.

Then, as another mile marker passes, I straighten. Does it have to be fantasy?

Claire wants me to get out of my shell—and yeah, get over Aiden—so maybe part of my problem is that things are "unresolved" between us. At least on my part.

I know the whole "get him out of my system" thing is something that romance heroines—and heroes—use because they're in denial. But here's the thing. I'm not in denial. I know very clearly what I want and what I don't want.

I don't want a guy like him for the long haul. Playboys and charmers will *always* let you down. I learned that lesson well enough to not get fooled again. But I also can't deny my attraction. Especially since it's so rare. So if sleeping with him—if I'm reading the signals right—will help me realize he's not as great as I've built up in my head, then that'll be good. Right?

I nod my head, firm in my decision.

By now, we're entering the outskirts of Daytona Beach, and GPS directs us through the beachy neighborhood that'll spill us onto the main strip on the Atlantic side of the city. I've lived in Florida most of my life and never been here. But it feels familiar to other beach cities in its architecture. Just a different layout.

Surf shops, burger joints, and wacky signs here and there to draw in the tourists.

"There's a Viking!" Aiden says, pointing to the left, and a beat later Miss Google says, "Your destination is on the left."

Sure enough, a larger-than-life statue in blue pants with a round shield and horned helmet stands beside the front end of a longboat. We pull into the parking lot, and I realize the longboat's doing double-duty as the entrance to a low-slung building.

After posing for pics by the Viking, we get checked in and head to our room. Other than the Viking and longboat, everything else seems pretty normal—like a Florida hotel on the beach a couple of decades out of date.

I open the door to our room. It's a king. My heart does a slow *thump*, while my libido does a fist pump.

Aiden lets out a low whistle behind me. "The 80s called, and they want their decor back."

"Right?" I put my hand up to shield my eyes—the bedspread's a bright blue pattern with a red, tropical print bolster and matching spread folded at the bottom. A peek into the bathroom reveals a cream yellow counter.

I move deeper into the room. That king bed. I swear it grows in size as if perturbed I'm ignoring it. Or trying to. I quick-step past it. "But hey, we've got a view!"

Glass doors open to a small balcony. Below, a pool glows with underwater lights, revealing a twisting water slide. Beyond stretches darkness, obscuring the ocean. "Well. *Tomorrow* we'll have a view," I say, looking over my shoulder at Aiden. *I still don't see you, bed.*

"Are you one of those crack o' dawn types who'll want to see the sunrise?" He tosses his duffel bag on the floor and plops into a chair at a small round table.

"Heck no."

"Good." He slides down the chair, extending his long legs. The denim stretches and bunches in enticing places. "You hungry? We can explore the bar area, see what Vikings might lurk about, and grab something."

My "yes" might be a little too high-pitched. "Lemme just…freshen up." Nervousness lays claim to my stomach again, because this feels a lot like a date, and I've also decided something.

Something *big*.

I'm going to take a risk.

Risk that I'm correctly reading the signals.

I nab my toiletries.

He's a player, right? And it's clear I need a little fun in my life. *Thanks, Claire*. So I need to look at this situation differently. Instead of pushing him away because he's not a long-term guy, as well as being hurt that he wasn't interested in me that night, I need to be all *carpe diem* on his cute butt.

After all, that was my original intention the night we met. And now he *does* seem to want me. I think. And our short time together is ideal—two more days. *That* should be enough of a defining boundary that I can't—won't—read more into it. Won't start building expectations only to be let down. Just a fling.

No lie, the decision makes me a little lightheaded. I run a brush through my hair, brush my teeth, and touch up my makeup, not that I wear much. My hands might be a little shaky.

I exit the bathroom, patting the back of my head to make sure there are no rogue hairs poking out.

Aiden's gaze flicks super-quick up and down my body. He smiles. "You look nice."

My palms get all sweaty. "Thank you."

Then we have an excuse-me dance in the hallway as

we each try to pass the other, and all the while I'm acutely conscious of his nearness and what I hope will happen later tonight. Now my whole body feels like one big flame of awkward awareness.

Aiden takes his turn in the bathroom, and I'm heading back over to the balcony when my phone rings. Claire.

"Hey." I slide open the glass door. A cool breeze hits my face.

"Hey, seen any Vikings yet?"

"Ha ha." Behind me, the shower comes on in the bathroom. Heat chases up my spine as I picture what that means. Aiden. Naked. With water running down all that toned skin.

"Be honest. How many times have you drawn stabby pictures of me in your travel journal?"

Her question yanks me from my increasingly dirty thoughts. I laugh for real this time. "Actually, none."

There's a pause. "Wait. Is this Jane?"

I roll my eyes. "Yes."

"I don't know. You don't sound pissed at me. Is it possible you might be, gasp, enjoying yourself?"

I answer tentatively but honestly. "I think I am."

"Good. Where are you now?"

"W—" I quickly turn this into an "*I* just checked into the hotel. The view's great. Overlooks the beach. Can't wait to see it in the daylight."

"What'd you think of the stops today?"

I fill her in, and it feels weird to carve Aiden out of the retelling. But, yeah, she'd be throwing an epic WTF lecture at me right now if she knew who was with me. And while it is still a bit WTF, it's also something private right now, and I can't explain it to her. I'm not sure I can explain it to myself.

To redirect the convo, I ask, "So what's going on with your doppelganger?" There's a hurricane out in the Atlantic bearing down on the Bahamas. It's hurricane season, so that's not unusual. But this one's been dubbed Claire. Like any smart Floridian, I keep an eye on storms brewing in the Atlantic.

"Ha ha. She's being a weirdo. Did a full circle out there."

The shower shuts off, and the door opens behind me, but it takes a moment for me to think through what can happen. Sure enough, Aiden says, "Ready to go?"

I jump. Why, I don't know. His presence wasn't a surprise, and his voice shouldn't have been. Guilt?

Claire pounces. "Who's that?"

I don't answer, because I'm kinda doing a mental Muppet flail, trying to process seeing Aiden fresh out of shower (dressed, but still), his asking me a question I need to answer, and Claire overhearing. My delay has made Claire suspicious.

"Jane, do you have a man in your room?" She sounds downright excited.

At the same time, Aiden says, "Sorry. Didn't realize you were on the phone." He makes a bashful face.

"No!" I say in an explosion of breath. I'm answering Claire, but Aiden looks at me, puzzled, while he collects his wallet and room key, placing them in his back pocket.

"I thought you said you were in your room?"

I whip around to put my back to Aiden. "I was." I step onto the balcony to make it more of a fudge than an outright lie. "But I'm not anymore."

"So you're not getting lucky tonight?"

"Who knows. Night's still young, right?" I tease, knowing this will throw her off the scent.

"That's the attitude, girl. I'm glad this trip's working out." A horn blares in the background. "Listen, I gotta run, but what do you think about coming to Saturday's game before you head back? I know The Turd'll be there, but by then, you'll be over him, right? This'll be a good test."

One more day with Aiden. Before I can think too hard, I say, "Yeah, that sounds great."

She rattles off directions, with a promise to text me the event address, and hangs up. I reenter the room. Aiden's head is dipped downward, his thumbs flying along his phone screen. He looks as if he's in professional mode, and it throws me, which is weird—the man *does* own a business.

Had I just assumed he was frivolous with it too?

He looks up then and smiles, the professional mask gone. "Ready for dinner?"

"Yes." *I think*, remembering my newfound resolution to be open to sleeping with him. I can do this.

10

Jane

Soon we're downstairs, and it doesn't take us long to discover that this place has no restaurant for dinner, nor does it have a bar.

"I think Rollo the Viking would have objected to this," Aiden grumbles.

We hike down the street a block or two to a pizzeria the front desk told us about. It's super casual, thank God, both because of how we're dressed, and also if it was romantic, my nerves would register on the Richter scale.

We split a pizza brimming with cheese, sliced tomatoes, and Italian sausage, as well as a bottle of Pinot Noir.

I set my empty wine glass down. *Hoo boy*. I might be a little buzzed from just two glasses.

"So what made you want to be a librarian?" He sits back and stretches his arm against the back of the red vinyl booth.

I tuck my napkin under my plate. "I'm sure you can guess."

"You love books."

"Yes."

"But why a library? Instead of working in a bookstore or working for a book publisher or something."

"I think I just love libraries, to be honest. The old one here was practically a babysitter for me." I look off to the side as memories well up. "My mom would drop my older brother and me off there while she ran errands. Do you remember the old library?"

"With the crazy steps?"

"Yes!" The riser-less steps rose from the center of the main lobby and went up, but skewed sideways. It was like an Escher drawing, though I didn't know the term at the time. Walking up them was a mind-bender, for sure.

I lean forward. "I would pretend I was a spy, and I'd sit in the upstairs areas and snoop on the people below, taking notes. If I went to the bathroom, I'd look at the shoes of the lady in the stall next to me and then make a game of trying to find her in the library.

"There were whole worlds in that place, with both the books and the people-watching. I loved it. I still remember one sci-fi book in a spinner rack that I started to read about some girl whose mind was able to exist in alternate planes, and I had to put it down because it was time to go. I've never come across it again, and I don't remember the title. But that's what a lot of my afternoons were like in the summer—people-watching and dipping into exciting worlds between covers."

And then I stop. Because—*holy cow*—I think that's the longest monologue I've had with him, and it was pretty dang dorky. I watch him, expecting him to say something patronizing like, "That's nice."

He smiles. "That's nice."

I scoff. Typical.

His eyes go wide, and he stretches his hand across the table, clasping mine near the empty wine glass. His skin's warm against mine, and just that little touch makes my breath catch.

"I mean it," he says. "It's an awesome memory. Magical. I didn't mean it to sound patronizing, though I can see how it could come across that way."

I'm not quite convinced, but he gives my hand a squeeze, and that warmth from his skin and his voice shoots through me. God, his brown eyes are looking intently at me, and I think…I think he means it. Screw it. I'll take him at face value. If he's lying, it'll be his fault if he's bored.

"It *was* magical. I hate that it's mothballed and scheduled for demo. But it was that experience that inspired me to create that kind of environment for others."

His hand's still on mine, and I don't dare move.

Act casual. Cuz, yeah, I'm *totally* used to discussing books with a hot guy, who's holding my hand. I can't even tell you how he looks to me right now—his arms create a ninety-degree angle, one stretched to hold my hand along the edge of the table, the other across the back of the booth. Since he's at the edge, it's as if he's blocking everyone out but me. And at the center of all this? Charcoal gray T-shirt stretched across his broad shoulders against the wine-red booth vinyl. His intense gaze focused on me.

"We had a good library where I grew up too. Dad always took us to their annual sale, and getting a library card was like a rite of passage."

"It was!" He understands.

His hand is still on mine, its warmth furling inside and combining with the glow from the wine. Oh wow. I think… I think the night's going well.

Aiden

I gently squeeze Jane's hand. "You ready to get out of here? We could work off our pizza with a walk on the beach."

Jane does her stillness thing, and I hold my breath. I don't want to push her. At all. I'm happy to have this evening go however she wants. Earlier, I showered and squeezed one off so I wouldn't be too amped. Her eyes widen a fraction, but she nods.

I stand, still holding her hand, and help her up. We split the bill at the counter and make our way back across and down the street. I seek her hand beside mine and thread our fingers together. She says nothing, and I sure as hell don't either. I've found that with Jane, it's best to let some things run under the surface or she'll spook.

The thing is, I've decided to explore this with her. And I don't just mean sex. So all this hand-holding and walk-on-the-beach thing isn't me being a smooth schmuck trying to get in her pants. I can't believe I'm about to voice this but—I'd like to *date* her.

So, to me, this is Date One.

I have no expectations for the night other than getting to know her better.

And because I'm suddenly girlishly giddy with that idea, I pull her hand up when we step onto the curb and give her knuckles a quick kiss. "That was a good pizza."

"It was. Just the right amount of cheese and sauce and a firm crust."

"Yeah, can't stand the limp ones."

"That's what she said."

I bark a laugh. It's an overused joke, but it's so unexpected from her. She gives a little giggle, and that lights me up.

"So what made you want to open a bar?"

"You showed me yours, so I show you mine, is that it?"

"Yes."

By now we've passed the hotels, and the moonlit beach stretches ahead, the steady rumble of the waves sloshing against the shore.

"Nothing as noble as yours," I answer.

Some people are grouped under an umbrella to the left, so we turn right and angle toward the waves. With my free hand, I take off my flip-flops, and she does the same. The sand is cool against my feet.

She nudges my arm with her shoulder. "Come on, you had to have had some reason. Running a bar isn't easy."

"No, it's not." And with a jolt, I realize that not once have I thought about the Butt since this morning's phone call. I'm tempted to call my manager again, but I have to trust he'd call me if another crisis happened. "Won the Quota license in a poker game."

"Wait. What? Quota?"

"Yeah. Was playing some high-stake games back in San Francisco with some tech guys. One couldn't afford the next ante, so he threw it in."

"I don't understand how that relates to the bar?"

I explain how Florida works on a quota system for selling liquor. Beer and wine? Apply to the state, no prob. Wanna sell liquor? Nope. No licenses left. So they go for big bucks in the private sector. This guy had inherited his from an uncle or something.

At first, when I won it, I didn't have plans. I was still happily engaged, working a job I loved.

But when Brittany left and I came across it while packing up to move?

It seemed like the answer to my fucking prayer to have a fresh start somewhere very different.

"I also love mixing drinks, the art of it, and have wanted to introduce signature drinks, but..."

"But your clientele isn't quite right for that, I take it."

"No. It's a beer and peanuts kind of place, and not even a craft beer kind of place. They just want the standard stuff. Nothing fancy. My Quota license is wasted on them."

"That sucks."

"Yeah." We step around an elaborate sand sculpture of what looks like a great ape. "When this one is settled enough, I'll branch out with a second one, use my Quota license, and switch the Butt to just beer and wine. Maybe on Osprey. Serve drinks that are family recipes of mine and my employees. Or maybe ones from locals."

"Ooh, that sounds like a cool concept, if you play up that part."

"Yeah. I want to use my uncle's Old-Fashioned recipe.

He's from an old Virginia family, and their recipe is a tad different. It's that difference that started my fascination with the vintage cocktails—how each one got passed down and how they vary."

We turn back at a curve in the beach and angle toward the lodge. She asks probing questions about the bar and my love for heirloom cocktails. I'm enjoying being in her presence and *talking*. It's a new experience for me. Well, not quite new, but it's been a long time since I've let myself have this kind of space with a woman I'm attracted to.

We're still holding hands, and I'm not sure if she realizes it, but she's swinging them back and forth as we stroll along the beach.

At the water spigot, we wash our feet and squish along in our flip-flops back up to the hotel.

We step into the elevator, and when the doors close, we're inhabiting a new kind of quiet space. Holy shit, I'm *nervous*. We're on our way up to a room that we're sharing—an artificial circumstance that wouldn't have occurred naturally if this was Date One. I don't want to make her feel uncomfortable, and I also don't want to fuck things up.

I turn to her, ready to say…something. Not sure what, but I open my mouth to articulate what's spinning through my head, what's knotting my stomach, and I stop. Because she's looking at me, eyes intense, with a whole 'nother quiet level. It's similar to the one where she rubbed her hands on the steering wheel, working up the nerve to say we could share her room. She wants to break out, like then, but this quiet is reverberating with much more power.

I'm fascinated. Rooted to the spot. Watching her.

11

Aiden

Holy shit. I feel as if I'm watching someone hatch out of their shell. Jane takes a step toward me. And another.

And then she, well…*throws* herself on me. Honest to God.

I catch her and fall back against the elevator wall with an *oof*. Her hand twisted into my T-shirt, she pulls me down, and our mouths crash.

Fuck yeah. All of my pent-up need for this woman unleashes in that moment, whipping through me. I wrap an arm around her and hike her up, molding her curves against me. Jesus, she feels fantastic. Soft parts to my hard—very hard—parts. We both groan, our mouths tasting, devouring. I stroke my tongue inside her, and she meets me, stroke for stroke. And, fuck, I didn't imagine her taste—she's got this intoxicating combo of sweet and spicy, laced tonight with our wine. I spin us around and get her in just the right—*unhh*—spot, but just as I press her against the elevator wall and she wraps her legs around me, the door dings.

I break our kiss long enough to stumble out of the elevator. She's not deterred in the least. Her hot little hands smooth over my shoulders, and she trails kisses down my neck. I lurch down the hall and aim for the room, when I just want to shove her against the wall right then and there and grind my hips into hers. Taste her mouth again. Oh God. Taste…

Family hotel. Family hotel. I repeat this over and over and fumble a key card into the slot. All the while, she's kissing me everywhere she can reach, her legs still wrapped tight around my waist.

When the door clicks shut behind us, it's like the starting flag at a race for me.

I push her up against the wall and tilt my aching cock into her. It's not enough, not near enough with the clothes between us, but we still. Then our heads slowly move until we're staring at each other.

And honest to God, it feels as if everything else stills too—the furniture, the air, the light. The moment.

But not our breaths. Oh no.

In the stillness, I rotate against her again. A real slow flex of my hips, and I watch her. Her eyes round and dilate, and her cheeks flush. I cradle her face with my hands and push against her again. Lust barrels through me, concentrating in my hard-as-a-rock dick. Sensuous heat curls in my lower back, tightening my balls.

She breaks the silence with a breathy, "Oh my God."

Yeah. No shit. Because I'm about to blow, and all I've done is grind myself against her like three times. I'm afraid to count cuz it might only be twice.

Jesus.

I think, deep down, I knew it was going to be like this. Perhaps that's why I kept it casual that first night. We needed to give this…this attraction room to ease out, little by little, like easing the air from a balloon instead of letting it immediately explode.

A fierceness lights up her eyes, which is hot as fuck. She curls her fingers into the fabric on my back and yanks up on my T-shirt. Totally on board. I pop my head out of the shirt hole and toss it to the floor.

But instead of yanking on her shirt and tossing it to the floor like I really really want to, like my fingers ache to do, I plant my hands on the wall on either side of her face. And take a deep breath. Maybe if my hands are there, and not on her warm, smooth skin I can maintain *some* kind of control.

Because I also know, deep down, she needs to lead this encounter.

Jane

AIDEN'S PALMS SLAP against the wall by my head, bunching his muscles all along his forearms and biceps. His bare chest is now on full display, though it's shadowed from the scant light filtering through the window.

Holy shit. He's magnificent.

If I could grab my Polaroid without breaking this moment—and if the flash wouldn't ruin the lighting—this sight would make a wonderful portrait. Shadowed light cuts across masculine planes and angles and muscles.

The sight also has me shaking with need. It has the potential to freak me out if I think too hard. Because, holy hell, I feel as if I've unleashed something powerful, not only with him, but in myself.

And the thrill of it is almost equal to the need. Almost.

I've never, ever been this attracted to someone.

I need to be careful, though. I can't read more into this than what it is.

Sex.

And I want that. With him.

Hence the reason I jumped him in the elevator.

I tighten my legs around his waist, relishing how he fits so perfectly against me, pressing against the part of me that's now aching for him.

Aiden's chest expands out and in as he takes measured

breaths, and I reach up and drag my fingers along the tendons standing out on his forearms. A work of art in flesh. That I can *touch*.

He closes his eyes and drops his head back slightly, which only draws attention to the perfect lines of his neck, the Adam's apple that bounces up and back down on a swallow, the stark lines of his collarbone topping his pecs.

All of it—all of it—acts like a frame to his impressive chest. The huge beefcake kind of guys don't put the zing in my thing, but I do like the power and definition of Aiden's muscles. A sprinkling of hair teases his nipples, then gathers in a line from there, in ever increasing darkness, straight down to his low-slung jeans.

A happy trail indeed.

And this is all for me, apparently.

At least for tonight.

And that's all I want, I tell myself.

And you know what? This gives me the freedom to be exactly who I want to be right now.

And right now, I want to be the woman who rakes her fingers down that chest and sees what happens.

I lightly scrape my short nails around his nipples, which surprisingly peak a teensy bit. Wow. He inhales sharply, and his stomach contracts, showing me that he's sporting at least a four-pack.

While I trail my fingers across his taut skin, he slowly rolls his hips against me, a steady beat like the waves pushing against the shore on the other side of the window.

I pinch a nipple, and his whole body jerks against me. He drops his head to mine, but his mouth stops shy of touching my lips, his breaths skimming my skin on each exhale. I knead along his pecs and close the distance, nipping his bottom lip. Tasting.

He grinds his hips against me more urgently, and our mouths clash, nipping, dipping, exploring. I swear to God, I feel as if my whole body is alive. Alive and excited. I want him *closer*. I push my hands around to his back, running up and down, and try to mold him tighter to me.

On a gasp, he tears his mouth away and rests his forehead against mine. "I can't," he rasps. "I can't anymore."

Oh *God*. Boneless with horror, my legs slip from around his waist, dropping my feet to the floor. I've misread *everything* and pushed myself on him…all unwanted. I'm no better than men who force themselves on women.

But then the next instant, I'm being pushed up the wall, and his hands are fitted around my waist, gripping tight. His mouth collides with mine, taking and taking, and my body lights up all over again, though I'm still confused as hell.

He breaks our kiss again. "Clothes. Off." His voice is husky with desire and urgency.

"I thought…I thought you just said you can't do this."

He stares at me, his eyes wild, though clouded with confusion. Then they clear and seem to glow more intently. "No. Jesus, no. I can't *hold back* anymore, letting you lead. I tried. I want you. I want you so fucking much."

"Oh. Oh!"

And in the soft glow of the ambient light, I tremble in anticipation as I slowly peel my shirt up.

Through the fabric, I can hear him breathing. When my shirt plops to the floor, he says, "Whoa," his voice…reverent? His strong hands skim up my waist, raising goosebumps in their wake. "I need to see you better. It's too dark right here."

Before I can respond, he grips my hips and marches me backward toward the bed. The whole time, his hooded gaze is darting all over me.

I'm wearing a plain white bra, but he's taking me in as if I'm sporting a Victoria's Secret number. A thrill runs through me that he sees me as sexy.

This hunk. Sees *me* as sexy.

My calves hit the back of the bed, and I buckle and fall flat against the firm mattress. I don't know what animates me, maybe my promise to be exactly what I want to be right now, but before I even recognize what I'm doing, I'm holding his gaze and unbuttoning the top button of my Capris.

His eyes flare with heat, and he avidly watches my unsteady fingers unbutton the clasp and slowly unzip. His hands are flexing at his sides, doing amazing things to his tendons and muscles. Feminine power streaks through me, arrowing down my belly to pool in my sex.

I'm starting to wiggle the Capris down my hips, when he lurches down, grips the waistband, and whips them off. My panties follow a second later, and I gasp at the cool air hitting me. I'm wet.

He drops to his knees and gives me an apologetic smile. "Sorry. Told you I can't hold back anymore."

Don't hold back.

And then he pins my hips to the mattress with his strong hands, his thumbs smoothing back and forth along my skin. Oh wow. I feel so exposed and…desired.

He circles my belly button with his nose, the short puffs of his breath tickling my skin, and I arch my hips.

"I've got you, baby," he whispers. He traces his tongue along my skin as his hands leave my hips and brush down my thighs. I clench in anticipation. He grips my knees and pushes my legs apart, and I swear to God, I almost break apart right then.

I shudder, and my hips buck as urgency races through me. Oh God, I want… I want to push myself on him, or… or touch myself, push against my clit and relieve some of this building, delicious pressure.

Then his tongue is right there, and he flicks my swollen nub.

"Oh, shit." *More. Harder.*

He clasps my knees harder and spreads me wider. My nether lips part, and the cool air kisses my wetness, a sensation I don't think I've ever felt. He hums in appreciation and sucks hard on my clit, and that's all it takes.

"Aiden!"

Heat and pleasure bursts through me, and I shatter. The tension releases me, and I start to relax, but he's nuzzling and licking and sucking, and I gasp as the tension snaps right back to my clit and everything in me tightens again, coiling. Holy cow, how is this possible? I arch my hips because it's too much and not enough.

He groans, and his velvety tongue delves inside me, and then he's back teasing my clit as if it's his only mission in life. And it's working, cuz, *ohmygod*, liquid heat is coiling coiling coiling. One hand leaves my knee, and I feel a blunt finger, and then two, stretch, then curl into me—the invasion that my body craves but not enough. All the while, he keeps flicking his gaze up to me, watching, gauging. And I'm riveted, watching him pleasure me as another orgasm is right, right, almost, *yes*, right there, and bam, that liquid heat tightens then bursts inside me. I'm shaking and gasping and going, "Aiden, Aiden, Aiden."

My brain's signaling *grab him, drag him up*, but I'm like a limp noodle on the bed as I ride out the aftershocks.

Holy, holy shit.

I've had guys go down on me before. Sadly, not a great percentage. Okay, I've only had sex with three different guys before. All of them long-term boyfriends, and only one would occasionally, begrudgingly do it. As if it was the price he had to pay to get me to reciprocate.

I never came from those few occasions, and to save ourselves from the time and energy it would take for him to get me off, I usually pulled him up after a minute or two.

But this? Holy shit. Not only was I not thinking or worried about how much work it was going to take to get me off that way, and should I stop him before he starts feeling bad about that, and, and, and everything else my mind usually throws into the moment, but I was also keenly aware that he was doing this because *he* was enjoying it too.

I open my mouth to say all this, then close it, my normal second-guessing making a belated appearance in this room with us.

He skims his amazing hands up my thighs and hips and grasps my waist. He gently squeezes. "What is it?" he whispers.

12

Jane

I squirm at Aiden's question, but I remember my promise to myself. "That's the first time a guy's gotten me off that way."

His eyes flare with heat again. "You're killing me, baby. For real?" Need seems to stretch his voice darker.

"Yes," I whisper.

"Shit, you just made me feel like Superman."

I giggle. "Supermouth."

He gives a huge grin. "Supermouth. I like that." He drops a kiss onto my belly, then another a little lower. He glances up at me, eyes swear-to-God twinkling. "Let's see if I can do it again."

He licks, long and firm, along my seam. "You seemed to like it best when I did this." He closes his lips around my clit and sucks hard. I buck.

"Yes." My voice comes out all breathy.

"And this." He presses his tongue hard on my nub and gives it a languorous roll. Heat and pleasure build again, but this time, I know not only will he succeed, but also that I don't want him to. I want him inside me when I come next.

His fingers and tongue are skilled, yeah, but I'm feeling a different ache, one that will only be satisfied when he fills me completely and moves inside me.

But God, I also want to touch *him*. Explore him. This could be my only chance. In fact, I know it is.

It might be the only time this new sexual confidence animates me.

And I want to make him feel good. But he's on his knees between my legs as if he'd rather not be anywhere else.

I slide my butt off the bed, startling him, and drop down to my knees in front of him. He falls back, bracing himself against the floor with one hand, and I take the opportunity to pull at his belt buckle. He's hard, straining against his jeans.

He pushes his hips forward and takes a sharp breath. Still stretched back and holding himself up with one arm, he reaches forward and grips my waist as his smoldering eyes avidly watch my fingers. I yank his zipper down, and he gasps. "Careful, baby."

He rises back up on his knees, making his stomach muscles contract. He cradles my face and brushes a soft kiss across my lips. I eagerly kiss back, shove his jeans down to his knees, and drag my fingers down the small of his back, tunneling under the waistband of his boxer briefs. Warm, firm glutes fill my palms.

God, his backside. I grip it, giving it a good, meaty squeeze, and he moans into my mouth, his kisses more urgent.

I shove his boxers down, but they bounce when I tug. Combining that with his pained groan with each tug, I realize they're hung up on his erection. I can't see what I'm doing, so I pat around and extricate him. Then my hand wraps around his firm, hard length.

His hips buck, and he hisses against my lips. He holds me more firmly, but his kisses have become distracted. Oh wow. I'm affecting him. *Me*. My ego plumps up a bit, and my libido gives me a high five.

He gives up altogether, resting his forehead against mine, his breaths uneven but warm against my cheeks. Now I'm able to glance down. My pale hand's gripping him, and, whoa, he's easily the biggest guy I've ever been with. I drag my thumb over the swollen tip and smear a bead of moisture.

I've never enjoyed giving head, mainly because my boyfriends would immediately push my head in that direction whenever we got hot and heavy and half undressed. I'd be like, yeah, yeah, yeah, I get the not-so-subtle hint, but also because I felt so inadequate to the task. Somehow guys want you to both be experienced enough to know what to do, but at the same time they don't like the idea of girls having experience in bed. I never understood that. So yep, I always felt this pressure to perform, which robbed the whole experience of any pleasure.

But now, for the first time, I *want* to taste him. See how far I can push this newfound sexual confidence. Maybe I'll be able to make him feel as good as he made me feel.

But my back is to the bed, and I have no room to maneuver. I grip him tighter and start to rise. "On the bed," I say.

"Yes, ma'am," he says on a whoosh.

Oh. God. I'm practically pulling him up by his dick.

I'm such a dork.

I let go, and he launches himself up onto the mattress, the movement morphing into an ungraceful dive as his feet tangle in his jeans and boxers.

He curses and kicks his feet in an attempt to free them, but I giggle, because I think it's adorable.

I yank them from his feet and bounce onto the bed. And then I gasp, because I'm finally able to see him in all his naked glory.

Corded thigh muscles, that V-shaped muscle by his hips framing the erection pressed tightly against his muscled abs. The pecs. The biceps.

My throat goes dry. Holy wow.

I glance up to his face, and he's watching me intently, his gaze hooded. I can tell he's about two seconds away from snatching me up, so I lean down and stroke a tongue slowly up his hard length.

He jerks, and his fingers tunnel into my hair, but he doesn't hold me in place or take over. I'm in control. Which I so appreciate. He arches his hips, though, as if he can't help it.

God, he's beautiful.

I lick him again, this time around the tip, and am rewarded with another lift of his hips. I part my lips and slide down while I grip him at the base and stroke up. He moans. His fingers jerk against my scalp. And his scent surrounds me, intoxicates. I breathe in through my nose and give another suck and swirl, relishing how he seems to grow in my mouth, and I think, I'm *enjoying* this. It's turning me on, and based on his reaction, I'm not doing too shabby.

Until he says, "Yes, just like that, baby. A little tighter."

I pop free, my heart hammering in mortification. "I'm sorry. I'm not very good at this." My words come out super-fast.

He jackknifes up, eyes wild. "God, baby, you're doing just fine. You have no idea."

Lord help me, he seems sincere. I bite my lip. I'm still holding him, and I grip tighter and pump once. He hisses in. "*Erngunk-unh*, like that. And I loved the swirly bit you did with your tongue."

"Yeah?" I say with more confidence.

He must hear something I didn't intend to reveal, because his gaze latches onto mine, questioning.

He cups my cheek, his palm warm and soft against my skin. It's such a tender gesture, I swear I almost forget myself and get all gooey. "I'm just letting you know what I like. It's not a criticism. Believe me. Jesus. I think you could just suck on me once more and I'd go off."

Really?

And then I truly listen. Listen to what he's saying. And flash back to him working me with his mouth and how he looked at me, watching. Oh wow. He wasn't Supermouth from knowing the exact technique to use with *any* woman. He was adjusting to what turned *me* on.

Then anger swells within me. Anger at my past boyfriends for making me guess what turned them on, making me think there was some skill I should magically know to apply.

And the anger disappears in a puff, because *I* should have

realized there was no shame in asking. Everyone's different. It's okay to *not know*.

And now I *really* want to know what turns *him* on. I hold his gaze and lick around his engorged head, running my tongue across the little slit at the top. A spicy saltiness pops my taste buds. His tip has a soft plumpness that's such a contrast to the rest of his cock. This time I take him deeper into my throat and swirl around with my tongue, gripping him tighter with my hand. He falls back against the bed with a moan. *Yes.* I pay attention to his movements, the noises he makes, and adjust. Again, excitement courses through me, and heat coils in my core.

But I feel as if I barely get started before he gasps and clasps my shoulders, his fingers digging in. "Told you. About to blow," he says as he pops me off his dick.

"Isn't that good?"

"Only if I want you to think I have the control of a teenage boy. Plus, Jesus—" He drops his head back against the pillow, his eyes shutting tight. "I want to be inside you. So bad." His eyes snap open, and he pins me with a fevered gaze. His Adam's apple bobs. "But only if you want that. Oh, God. Do you want that? Please say you want that."

I laugh and throw a leg around his narrow waist. Going by instinct now, because I'm always too much in my head *worrying* whenever I have sex, I place myself right over him and let my wet sex glide up his hot length and then back down. I shudder. "Yes. I want that." So much.

"Thank God." He sits up, his hand stretching toward his jeans at the end of the bed, but then he plops down with a choked gasp because I'm sliding up and down him again. I can't help it, okay? He groans, and I thrill.

I nab his jeans, and he snatches them from me. He shudders as he pulls out his wallet and fishes out a condom. "I don't think I can get this on fast enough."

The foil packet crinkles as he rips it open. I ease back to give him room, and he deftly sheathes himself. Before I can move again, he grasps my waist and lifts me straight into the air. He's still curled up into what's basically a sit-up, his stomach muscles tight. The sight of him below me, his erection so hard it's lying flat against that taut belly, has me thrashing my legs a little, I won't lie. Anticipation coils its heat in my stomach.

"Ready?" he asks.

"Yes."

"Line me up, baby," he rumbles.

Oh yeah, he can't do that with his hands occupied. I like this giving-directions thing. I ease him forward, and he lowers me until the broad tip nudges my opening. And just that brief touch, that tiny pressure, has me shaking in anticipation. Deep inside, that ache to be filled grows.

Why is he pausing? I glance up to his gorgeous face, and his sinful eyes are already there, waiting, watching. Our gazes lock.

"I want you kissing me when I lower you." His voice is like liquid sex, velvety, molten, urgent. "I want to be kissing you when I feel you around me for the first time."

God. I could easily fall for this man.

Just sex. Just sex.

I cradle his face, my fingers brushing against the sharp lines of his jaw, his scruff, and I brush my lips against his soft, full ones. He moans into my mouth and lowers me, stretching me, inch by scorching inch. Our kisses become frantic. Our tongues tangle and stroke, and then he slams me fully down onto all that hot—oh wow—hardness.

I gasp against his mouth and arch my head back, because holy shit, the feeling is exquisite. He's huge, and I'm full of every hot inch of him, stretching me. I tremble, urgency gripping me, centered where we're joined. Oh God, if one of us moves, I'll orgasm. I swear. Though moving might not be possible yet anyway, because yeah, he's huge and I need to adjust.

It's a sweet, sweet ache.

His tantalizing mouth is trailing feverish kisses across my neck, his lips soft and silky against my skin. I lean back farther, and a warm wetness tugs my nipple. I buck forward on a gasp, which causes him to shift deliciously inside me.

Aiden chuckles. "You like that?" He nips and teases. "Wow. Your breasts are..." He gives it a tweak between his fingers, then laves it with the flat of his tongue. I jerk and dig my fingers into his shoulders. "They're so sensitive."

I'm assuming that's a good thing. Yep. That's what I'm going with.

He cups my breast, plumping it to his mouth, and sucks and sucks and sucks, and oh my God, I'm now frenzied. I am. I'm moving on him now. Adjustment period, bye-bye. My movements are jerky as I ride his girth in short pumps because I don't want him to stop suckling my breast. He's kneading and sucking, and the pleasure is like a direct link between his heavenly mouth and where I'm sliding up and down him, the hunger zinging down, the friction everything, everything, holy shit.

A low spasm grips me, different from when I pleasure myself. *This* has its sensuous claws in me, like it's not going to just go poof and disappear. No, this is a deep, shuddering pull. I grip his shoulders tight and just let it come let it come, and then it's on me, a searing climax that blasts through my whole body. I'm shaking, and my mind goes flat for a second, though I'm aware enough to hear Aiden pant, "Holy fuck."

He cinches his arms tight around me and goes completely still. Then his cock, buried deep inside me, jerks, and because we're holding each other so firmly, I can feel his whole body slightly tremble.

Blood is pounding so hard through me, it feels like a marching band, and we're trying to catch our breath. Our skin is covered in a light sheen of sweat.

And all my mind can do is say *oh wow* over and over again.

13

Aiden

I slip back into our room, juggling the tray loaded with breakfast I nabbed from downstairs and trying to be quiet. When I left Jane a few minutes ago, she was conked out. Adorable and all mussed, twisted in the sheets, her hair in disarray, but conked out just the same.

I grin. Because she still is.

There's also less tension in my shoulders—on the elevator ride down, I logged into my bar's bank to check the daily deposits. Not only are the credit card totals like I'd expect, so are the cash deposits. Stuart's definitely a keeper.

I ease the tray onto the room's round table, wincing when it makes a slight *dink*. I hurriedly glance over my shoulder, but she's still stretched out on her stomach, the sheets only covering her legs. Her delectable ass is pointing right at me.

God, my hands itch to graze along that smooth, soft skin again. Grip that ass tight. Squeeze. Let go, and then squeeze again. Yeah, I'm an ass man. And Jane has a perfectly rounded ass. An ass that sits up high and proud. I crumple the note I left on the nightstand in case she woke up, quickly strip, and slip back under the sheets. The bed's barely had time to cool—I was that fast getting breakfast.

No way did I want to miss waking up with her beside

me. Or worse, her waking up and panicking at my absence. Cuz I think she'd panic. I would, and I don't care if that makes me a mushy wuss.

I burrow up beside her. The beautiful lines of her back are to me, so I slip an arm—reaaalll slow—around her waist and nuzzle up behind her with a steady movement. I don't want to wake her yet. I want her to wake up in my arms.

Yeah, cheesy, I know. But fuck it.

I shift that last distance and, ah, yes. She fits so perfectly against me. Her hair's floral scent fills me, its strands soft against my nose and lips.

Having her ass pinned to me, my nose in the perfect spot, my hand skimming up her soft, smooth stomach and oh so stealthily resting against one of her beautiful boobs doesn't make me harden.

Nope.

That fucker's been hard since I woke up to find my dick happily wedged against her ass.

It only got happier—and harder—as my brain came on line and splashed me with all of last night's erotic memories.

A sleepy moan escapes her, and she wiggles her butt, nudging my very happy dick. Impossibly, it swells even more.

I'm a healthy, red-blooded, heterosexual male, so my reaction's not newsworthy. We're pretty simple with the biological imperative and all—female ass pressed to our dick? It's going to harden, just sayin'.

But what's different is how much more quickly and how much more intense it is with Jane. There's an extra animating force layered through our interactions. Chemistry. And, Jesus, did that chemistry flare and feed off us last night.

With what I'm about to admit, if I shared it with Luke, Conor, or any of my other buddies, they'd yank my man card away so fast it would cut. But the truth is, with her I feel a *tenderness*.

I likened her vulnerability before to a hot potato I was afraid I'd mishandle. Now a need surges through me. A need to slip on heat-resistant gloves so I *can* handle her. Protect her.

That's new.

Paired with that feeling, though, is a primal urge to fuck her. Over and over. All day. Like bunnies. And I can't even fathom ever getting tired of her.

And that right there—all of it—should scare the shit out of me, but I can't seem to care.

Jane's breathing shifts. She stiffens slightly, but I tighten my arms around her and murmur, "Good morning," near her ear.

She shivers in my arms. And there it is. The first spark in our chemistry's chain reaction. It coils and strengthens between us.

"Morning," she replies, her voice soft and husky.

Which Jane will appear this morning? Will she try to ghost me again? Did I fuck things up by going too fast last night?

Before that worry can take root, she nudges that nicely rounded ass against my cock.

Fuck, yeah. I didn't want to be a needy bastard and push for another round this morning, but that's a clear signal. And I'm going to heed it.

I part my fingers over her nipple and skim down the luscious slope of her breast. Slow, though, because I want to draw out this moment. Her skin pebbles as I return to her responsive nipple and lightly stroke back and forth, back and forth. Her little nub hardens under my fingers.

Jesus. Last night. Her riding me with such abandon. So fucking hot. I had no hope of making it last. As one of the strongest orgasms I've ever had smacked me, I had room for only one thought—thank the Orgasm Gods she'd come. Or I'd have failed her spectacularly. Like her past lovers, it sounds like.

I clamp my fingers together, capturing her stiff nipple, and tug. She gasps. And my hip jerks. It's as if we're synched—I touch her, she reacts, and then I react. A feedback loop.

The more I tweak and knead and rev her up, the more

I'm revved up. Which completely screws with my plan to take this slow, because soon we're both gasping, my fingers are flicking and stroking her clit, our mouths are crashing into each other despite the awkward angle, and my hard-as-a-hammer cock is plunging between her thighs, aided by the slickness of her arousal.

Fuuuck. I want to be inside her. Now.

I clasp an arm around her waist, cup my junk against her with my other hand, twine my legs around hers, and roll us across the bed. Our feet get tangled in the sheets. She lets out a squeal and a throaty laugh. "What're you doing?"

"Getting us closer to the condoms!"

I fling an arm to the nightstand where I'd thrown the rest and snatch one. Our roll across the bed ended with her lying on top of me, her back to my chest. My dick jerks at a tentative touch, then a firmer one. I lift my head. Over the pale peaks of her boobs, I see she's extended her arm down, and her fingers are stroking the tip of my cock, which is pointing up through her supple thighs like a fucking flagpole. Her warm wet heat feels fantastic against my dick. As do her featherlight touches.

Now she's moving my cock back and forth, the plump folds of her pussy slicking across me, but the visual makes me snort.

"What?" she asks.

"Looks like you're playing with a joystick."

"Well…if the nickname fits…" She hums and again rubs my dick against herself.

I can't help it, I bust out laughing. Before she can say anything further, I roll her to the side and sit up on my knees. She peers back over her shoulder, her eyes glinting with mischief and sexual confidence. God, I fucking love seeing that. Because I helped put it there.

Seconds later, I have the condom package ripped open, my cock straining, my balls tight up against me. God. I feel as if I haven't come in months.

She rolls onto her stomach and wiggles that pert, curvy

ass of hers, and I groan. I want to tell her to stop with the wiggle action, or I'm going to explode before I can even get the damn condom in place, but I don't. She might misinterpret. It's clear she's had lousy boyfriends and that this sexual confidence is new. I have no wish, no fucking wish at all, to squelch that.

That chest-beating feeling surges through me again, because I'm the lucky bastard who for some reason has the right compatibility to give her that confidence. Hell if I know what I did or said last night, but I'm delighted.

Fully sheathed, I swing my knee over her fuck-awesome legs, straddling her. I brush my hands around those tempting cheeks, her smooth, soft skin whispering across my palms. I grip her hips and yank her to her knees.

She arches her back, but her gaze is questioning. I slide my palm around her hip and stroke my finger through her wetness. She closes her eyes, groans, and pushes her hips toward me, and—fuck—I want to part her legs, shove myself into her warm heat, and pound us both to oblivion. But I resist.

God, somehow I resist.

I want to tease that clit of hers until she comes.

Fingers coated with her juices, I slick them down my condom-wrapped cock. I thrust my cock between her lush thighs and across her folds—with my knees trapping her legs together, it's a tight fit. It won't be enough pressure for her, but I tease her first by easing out and back across, reveling in the feel of her slicking across my cock.

She bucks. "Aiden," she whispers.

Her voice. Saying my name. I fucking love hearing it while I'm teasing her like this.

I lick the heel of my hand and press it hard against my cock on the next slide between her thighs, grinding it against her as I thrust. My girl likes pressure there, I've found. Hard pressure.

She gasps. "Aiden!" Her thighs start to shake. Almost there. On each retreat, I flick and stroke her swollen nub.

On each thrust, I push my dick hard into her clit with my hand. On the next flick-stroke, she cries out and shudders and comes, making my next pass easier through her thighs and the folds of her pussy.

Her responsiveness to me—it lights me up inside. And I feel confident it's me, because she revealed a lot last night with her confessions.

While she's still gasping, and her hands are rhythmically clenching and unclenching the pillow, I ease inside her on the next pass. Tight heat clamps around my dick, and I drop my head back and close my eyes. Tiny aftershocks of her orgasm are pulsing my cock. Honest to God, I almost explode right then and there.

As best I can, I smother the sensation. I want to make this last, dammit.

But my gaze is inevitably drawn back down. Back to where we're joined. Mistake. Because the sight of my cock easing out from between her thighs, coated with her juices, makes something primal surge through me. Liquid heat coils tighter as I slam back into her, gripping that delectable ass tight. I piston into her three times before I recapture my control and drag out.

I smooth my hand over her shapely hip, across her stomach, until my fingers reach the underside of her luscious breasts. I graze my fingers up and around those delicious curves and pinch her rigid nipple.

"You with me, baby?"

Her breaths are coming fast, making her breasts a delightful, jiggly handful. Her head hanging down, she nods jerkily. "Oh God, yes. Don't stop." Her voice is an octave lower than normal, and the sultry pitch tingles across my skin as if it's a touch all on its own.

"Don't plan to," I grit out.

Fuuuuck—I want to keep teasing her, but urgency pounds through my blood. Once I start moving in her again, I know I'll lose control. And I want her to come again before I do.

Desperate, I tweak her nipple and gather up the silky

brown hair falling around her face. I put my full concentration on the task, as if by doing so I'm also gathering the last shreds of my control. Every last hair tamed and in my fist, I twist it once around my fingers and clasp her naked shoulder, her hair held firmly in my grip. I don't want to hurt her, but I also want her hair out of the way, and this gives her options—if she wants it, she can have a slight sting.

I close my eyes, grit my teeth, and ease back inside her. We both moan. I make it as slow as I can, but it's killing me feeling her tight heat grip me as if it had already been missing me these few short minutes.

Clutching her shoulder and hip, I surrender to the need and thrust inside her over and over, watching her perky ass hit me as I bury myself in her each time. She arches her back even more, her head and shoulders now resting on the pillow. The sight of my cock disappearing into her from this new angle… Oh, fuck. I piston into her. I try to finesse my thrusts, giving my hips a slight twist so my tight-as-fuck balls can slap her sex, but I'm past knowing whether I'm accomplishing anything other than making her gasp and moan and call my name over and over.

On a hoarse cry, she trembles, and she slumps to the side, her sex milking me.

Oh, thank God.

I fall with her, covering her back, and she jackknifes her knee. I mirror the movement with mine, and the new angle gets me even deeper where I want. Deeper into Jane. I mold her back to my chest, and it only takes one more deep thrust for me to know it's over. I bury my face in her neck, and heat blasts along my lower back, tightens my balls, then explodes from me with such force that I stifle a shout against her sweet-sweaty skin, and my mind goes quiet and blank.

Slowly, awareness returns. I'm still buried deep inside her, and we're still panting. Our skin is slick with sweat, and my heart beats hard against her back.

Jesus Christ.

As I slowly bring my mind back online, I fall completely on my side, snugging her up against me, trying to keep myself inside her, though I'm growing softer by the second. I have to pull out soon and dispose of the condom, but…not yet.

I want to stay like this for a moment longer.

A truth bomb explodes my sensual haze.

By far, by fucking far, this is the best sex I've ever had. And because I'm an idiot, I say something completely unrelated. "I got breakfast."

She's slowly recovering her breath, but manages to say, "Good. I'm starving."

I pull her closer and kiss her shoulder.

14

Jane

I'm trying—desperately—to not read anything into the fact that not only did Aiden somehow procure breakfast while I was sleeping, he also remembered what I ate yesterday morning.

The oatmeal and hot tea were cold, but I warmed them in the microwave of our kitchenette.

Just as desperately, I'm trying to act all casual. As if it's completely normal for me to wake up next to him and have another bout of mind-blowing sex. And then sit down and have breakfast together on a balcony overlooking a pool and beach.

And not just a polite, sit across from each other at a table kind of breakfast.

Nope. No, siree.

I'm sitting in his lap, and his strong arms are wrapped around my waist, his chin on my shoulder, as we both look out through the balcony rail and watch late-morning walkers along the sand, kids running in and out of the surf, and preteens trying, and failing, to skim board. And I'm practically vibrating at the effort to cloak myself in this casual shell.

He ate his breakfast while I heated mine—one minute there was a plate of food in front of him, and the next it was gone. I suspect it's not nearly enough for him, but it was all he could bring up by himself.

I only have the banana left now, and I break off a chunk with my fingers and eat it, unwilling to bite into it myself. It's the way I always eat my bananas in public.

I expect him to be like a guy and make some remark, but he doesn't. He seems content to have me rest against him, with no conversation, as I fill my stomach. It's a great feeling.

It's also an unusual one to experience around others. Instead of feeling drained by being around him for such an extended period, I'm refreshed. Ready to start the day.

Typically, by now, even with my bestie Claire, I'd be feeling restless. I'd need to be alone to recharge. By degrees, I can feel myself ease into a true calm.

I break off the last bit of banana, hand it to him, and toss the peel onto the side table. I lick my fingers, and he tightens his arms.

"What's Claire got planned for us today? Do we have a site-packed day?" The way I'm pressed against him, I not only hear the words but also feel them rumble against my back.

"Actually, no. Just one site."

His hand moves up and cups my breast, and I shiver.

"I like the sound of that. How far away? Do we need to get started soon?"

"Nope. It's in Daytona Beach. Some place called Dunlawton Sugar Mill Gardens."

His chin lifts from my shoulder. "A botanical garden? That doesn't seem to fit the theme."

"You're right. It doesn't." I shift in his lap so I can see him. "That's because what we're actually supposed to see is located there. The Bongoland Ruins."

"What's that?"

A spurt of happiness buoys my voice. "I don't know."

He squeezes my breast. "Awesome."

We sit there, quiet, but together. He slowly kneads different parts of me—an elbow, a thigh, a wrist. And it doesn't feel like foreplay. More like a subconscious thing he's doing as we watch the day unfold along the beach. And I like it. I really really like it.

Every once in a while, one of us points out some antic on the beach, and we take guesses as to the perpetrator's backstory.

I even feel comfortable enough to tell him I'm going to paste in yesterday's pics into the journal, and he seems completely fine with me doing something separate from him. We move downstairs to a shady spot by the pool, and while I do the minimum required for the journal, he sits down at the pool's edge.

But as I tape in the last pic, the easiness starts to dissipate. And for the strangest reason. It's because I *am* so at ease. I'm forgetting that this is *just sex*.

And I can't forget that.

This is a fun interlude with a player. Nothing more.

Once I drop him off in Atlanta, this will all be over.

Aiden

Our steps slow as we exit the elevator at the Sun Viking Lodge and head to Jane's car. I'm reluctant to leave. It's as if, by moving slow enough, we can somehow keep the bubble we enjoyed in that room and have it travel with us, instead of making it burst by moving too quickly.

Fuck. I need my man card taken away.

I squeeze Jane's hand and nod to the sign labeled Viking Kafe. "Going to load up on some more grub."

"Good idea."

We purchase some muffins and fruit, as well as some bottled water, and head to the car.

Unfortunately, it's been baking in the sun for most of

the morning, so we open the doors while we toss in our bags.

We roll down the windows, and she reaches in and turns the key in the ignition to let the A/C crank for a bit before we get in.

This time it won't start.

Not even on the third try. "Pop the hood. Let me take a look."

She does, and I scoot around to the front of her car. I open it up. The cables running to her battery look secure, but there's a bit of crud built up on the ends. "I'll be right back. You have jumper cables, just in case?"

"Yes."

Soon I'm back with a can of Coke and a rag. I loosen the cables and pour the liquid over the crud and watch it dissolve. I clean the ends and secure them back in place. I lean out to the side. "Try it now."

She tries again, but no luck. She looks at me with a worried bite of her lip. "Jumper cables?"

"Yep. I'll see if I can find someone who'll give us a jump."

Shortly, I'm back with one of the hotel's maintenance men, and he maneuvers his truck into place.

The battery takes the jump—hallelujah—but the guy refuses a tip.

Soon we're heading south toward Bongoland, and I angle the A/C vent for maximum blowage. "The battery's only a year old?"

"Yep."

"Looks like you got a dud." I fish out my cell, type *auto stores* into Google Maps, and direct her to the nearest one. "We should get you a new one, just to be safe."

Twenty minutes later, I'm washing my hands in the store bathroom after having switched out her battery for a new one in the auto store parking lot. It's stupid, but I feel a bit of pride that I was able to do this for her.

Jane

We pull up at the entrance to the botanical garden, but the gates are closed. "Crap. I thought it'd be open."

Aiden has his phone out. "It says on the website it's open until five."

We get out of the car anyway and approach. That's when I see a smaller sign.

```
Closed for maintenance
today. Sorry for any incon-
venience.
```

Surprisingly, I'm disappointed.

But what can we do? Claire will understand. I lift the camera to take a picture of the sign as proof, and a warm hand clasps mine, staying me.

"Come on." Aiden glances at me with a mischievous smile and nods his head along the fence. "Let's walk the perimeter. Maybe we can see from here what Bongoland is."

We're about to step away from the gate, when I'm again pulled up short by Aiden's hand.

"Hello there," he shouts.

I whip around. Inside, a distance away, a figure is patrolling the grounds.

Aiden waves, and the figure changes direction and strides toward the gate. As the person nears, I can see it's a petite, trim woman in a guard's uniform.

"Terribly sorry," she says, "but we're closed today." Her blonde hair's cut in a bob that sways with her head shaking no.

Aiden steps closer to the gate and grips one of the bars. "I see. Any chance you can let us in?"

The timbre of his voice has changed, and I glance at him. He's smiling at the woman with his head at a slight angle.

The woman sighs, and, good Lord, her stance seems to go a little soft as she stares at Aiden in obvious appreciation. "Sorry. One of the employees called in sick. It wouldn't be an issue, except that we're already short staffed on account of Tammy up and quitting last week without notice."

"So you don't have enough staff around to watch all the visitors."

"That's right." Now her hair swishes forward from her nod.

"But what if you only let *us* in. We wouldn't be too much to handle. I promise."

"Well…" Her gaze darts to mine and back again.

And then Aiden engages his full charm mode, blasting the poor woman. "Please? I've promised my girlfriend a visit to Bongoland, and we're leaving today for Atlanta. I have this whole romantic picnic planned, which"—and here he looks at me with sheepish apology—"I just let slip." He's only missing a lip bite to effect the full-on oh-shucks look. And far from making him look like a pouty boy, he looks hot as hell.

The *awww* practically oozes from the guard's eyes.

She steps forward and unlocks the gate. "If it's just you two, and you promise to—"

"We'll be good," he quickly promises.

She tries to look stern, but it's clear she's fallen prey to his charm.

We step through, and Aiden winks. "You're the best. Thank you! Which way to Bongoland?"

The security guard rattles off directions, and we wend our way through a surprisingly well-maintained botanical garden with paths branching everywhere. The day is gorgeous, birds are chirping in the trees, and we stick to the shade.

"You're such a charmer. You had that poor guard almost turned into goo on the ground."

He winks at me. "Got us in, didn't it?"

I smile. "Yes." But an irrational jealousy has sprouted,

which is stupid because I have no claim on him. He can be charming to whomever he wants. I yank the poisonous feeling out of my heart before it can take root.

But wow, yeah—shit. That reaction. I couldn't have received a better warning if my heart had been wired with a warning bell. I've let myself read too much into what's going on between us. Seeing him put on that charm is a reminder. A good, well-timed reminder. Aiden's the playboy Claire warned me about.

He must pick up on my mood, because he nudges my shoulder, both eyebrows raised. "You okay?"

"Totally. Thanks for getting us in. So what are your guesses for what awaits us?" I ask, wanting to keep the mood light. Determined to be just what the occasion calls for. Nothing more.

15

Jane

We pass the time making outrageous guesses as the botanical garden unwinds from manicured paths to ones wild with Spanish moss-laced oaks, palmettos, and other scrub.

Aiden pulls our joined hands up and points. "Ummm. What the hell is *that?*"

We approach, and it's…a small concrete dinosaur in bad shape. Opposite, an old mechanical wheel and gears sit under a wooden roof.

Nearby, we find a path lined with big three-toed stone footprints painted green. A hand-painted sign announces, "Do Not Feed the Dinosaurs," with most of the word "Not" missing because of a big bite taken out of the sign.

"What the hell?" Aiden says, his voice amused.

We walk down the path, and then we see it. A huge concrete stegosaurus corralled by a black metal fence.

Oookaaaay.

I point. "There's another sign."

We sidle up to a sign that reads BONGOLAND in blocky letters and learn that this was a failed theme park in the early fifties.

"Concrete dinosaurs?" Aiden says.

"Apparently so. That was *not* one of our guesses."

He laughs. "No, it wasn't."

Apparently, it was named after a baboon on the premises, and there used to be a train that brought tourists around the theme park, which also featured a replica Seminole village and a human sundial. It closed from lack of interest.

We turn around, and there's a giant T-Rex.

"Its head," I say. "Oh my God."

"Well, the sign warned us that the guy did it to the best of his ability."

The body of the T-Rex is bad enough, with its legs almost looking like separate attachments on its sides. But the head… It's thin and narrow, and while it *does* have a lot of teeth, it looks like a dopey grin. It reminds me of the plaster horse at Solomon's castle.

I hand Aiden my Polaroid, try my best to imitate the grin the T-Rex is sporting, and he snaps a pic.

A sign nearby warns of the danger of the dinosaurs, with another big bite taken out.

We wander the paths and find one more, a Triceratops, all that's left of the old theme park.

It's quirky and sad.

I sit down on a nearby bench. "I picture this guy all excited about this theme park and how fantastic it will be. The crowds."

Aiden settles next to me and pulls out the muffins and fruit he bought earlier. "And then it's a flop." He passes me a muffin and a banana.

I peel the banana and look around. "Yeah. He and his friend put all this work into it, creating these dinosaurs to the 'best of their ability,' and wait for the crowds. Stay up nights talking about their big dream."

I don't know why it's affecting me so much. I just hate picturing the disappointment. Especially when it follows the excitement and hope of a new venture. There's something so vulnerable about that excitement that makes the disappointment brutal.

"Don't forget the train and the Seminole village they built."

We eat the rest of our food in silence.

Once we're done, Aiden stands and holds out a hand. "Come on, baby doll, let's see if we can find the human sundial."

I give a start at the nickname, but I put my hand in his, and he pulls me up.

"What was that?" he asks.

"What?"

"You went stiff and got a funny look on your face. We can skip the sundial."

I laugh. "No. It's not that. It's just that, that's what my dad calls me."

"Baby doll?"

"Yep."

He steps back. "Yikes. Yeah, I'll be skipping that one then." He laces his fingers with mine and picks up our trash that we'd stuffed in a plastic bag. "Good memory or bad?"

"The nickname?"

"Yeah."

I shrug. "Neither really. He's a lot like you, actually."

He groans. "That's not good. How so?" We start walking down the path, deeper into the property. An overhanging tree momentarily casts his face in shadow.

"He's a charmer."

"You think I'm charming?" he teases.

I give him a get-real look. "You know you are. You charmed us in here, didn't you?"

"Guilty as charged," he says, voice light, but I see a shadow cross his face, quickly masked.

It works out well for my mom. She adores my dad and vice versa. There's nothing he won't do for her.

But I learned pretty early on that charm is cheap. My dad would always pour it on thick whenever he failed to show up at a school recital like he promised or some such thing like that. He'd make other grand promises too…and never deliver. He would for mom, but not for me.

I don't think I was quite what either of them expected.

They both wanted a princess-type to dress up. Instead they got a mousy girl who'd rather bury herself in books or browse the aisle of an office supply store than a clothing store.

I was—and am—a third wheel in my own family.

Aiden

We don't find the human sundial, but we do find another necessary attraction, apparently, because Jane turns to me and holds out her Polaroid and journal.

"Watch these for me?" She thumbs behind her to the ladies' bathroom.

I toss the trash in the garbage by the building and take her things. "You trust me with your innermost secrets?" I hold up her journal and waggle my eyebrows in a mock-sinister expression.

She rolls her eyes. "Nothing secret in there. Look away."

She disappears inside, and I lean back against the building. I lift the journal. Hell, I'm as curious as the next guy, and she doesn't seem to care. I open to the last entry.

Even so, I don't read the captions. She said I could look, but it feels like a line I shouldn't cross.

I smile at the one I took of her by the giant Viking. She's doing a serious face, trying to look like the fierce warrior. It's as if each time she does these imitative poses, I see her peeking out from her shell. Being daring. Being herself.

And it's one hell of a turn-on. Because it's just like her transformation in bed.

I run my finger alongside a Polaroid of the restaurant where we ate last night, which led to the stroll on the beach, then the blistering hot sex and her calling me Supermouth and fiddling with my joystick.

I chuckle and flip back another page, and there she is in front of the giant potty chair, umbrella in hand, but half of her hair blocking her face from the wind and rain.

There's the one of her in front of the Spook Hill sign.

But as I flip back through the memories we'd made in such a short amount of time, something bothers me, and I can't quite name it.

I turn to another page, and it dawns on me.

Despite taking selfies of us together at each of our stops, every single memory she chose to record in the journal is of just her. Alone.

I push away from the wall, still looking at the one of her at Solomon's castle. This journey is about *her*, prompted by her friend Claire. It's *not* about me, or *us*, but...

An unwelcome hurt suffuses me, and I blow out a frustrated breath. I don't know, it just...feels strange that we explored these places together—hell, I even had to *push* her to spend more time at some of these—and it's as if I'm not even part of this trip. Not worth recording.

It's stupid, but I can't dislodge the feeling. As if she's ghosting me again, but this time, I'm the ghost.

The door creaks open just as I get to the first page, and I snap the journal shut.

Jane emerges with a big grin. "I've gotta take a pic of the inside."

"Of the bathroom?" I hold out the Polaroid.

She looks around, but of course no one's near. "Come see."

I peek inside the sanctum-sanctorum that is a woman's bathroom, but it looks pretty basic in its essentials. Except for the walls. They're covered in primitive but colorful drawings of dinosaurs.

She lines up a shot and takes her pic. I hand over her journal, and she stuffs the photo into the back. "Now, let's go find that sundial." She grins and pushes past me.

I shove aside my pity party and follow. This is *her* trip. I'm aided by the sight of her ass cupped in her Capri pants, and my dick gives a little, hello-there kick.

Deeper within the grounds we stumble across the remains of an old sugar mill. Explains the name of the botanical garden. We stroll along all the paths and outdoor exhibits, everything well-labeled, Jane fully engaged, but an antsiness has me by the short hairs, and I can't shake it.

I'm sure the site's interesting and historical and all that crap, but I can't focus. Not on it, at least. No, I'm focused on Jane. Focused on how she moves. Focused on how she interacts with everything we find.

It's as if we've reversed roles. Now she's the enthusiastic explorer of this site, and I'm the reluctant tag-along. But it's more than that. Today's Thursday. By this time tomorrow, we'll be in Atlanta. I'll be with my team, and she'll be turning around and heading back home. Our time's growing short, and that doesn't sit well with me. Not at all.

The more I watch her, and the more my role as a ghost on this trip sinks in, the more I want to insert myself. Make a big enough splash that she has no choice but to acknowledge my part in her journey. It's an immature reaction, I know.

But it's the only explanation for why, when we round the back of one of the sugar mill buildings, I grab her upper arm, push her up against the wall, and start kissing the shit out of her.

It's rough, and she'll push me away. Any moment now. Then—*oh fuck*—my sexy librarian groans into my mouth and grips the back of my head.

The semi I've been sporting all morning now pops against my jeans as if it's been zapped. I want to be inside her. Now.

I grip her waist and slide her up the wall so she's of the same height, and all the while we're nipping, stroking, tasting. She's gripping my hair so hard it stings. I push my hips against her, giving her a good hard grind and pinning her there, my aching cock against her pussy.

She gasps in my mouth, and her legs whip around my waist and squeeze. *Fuck yeah*. I trail desperate kisses down her neck, as I basically dry hump her. She's wiggling and writhing, and as before it's like zero to sixty between us.

16

Jane

Holy cow, there's nothing sexier than a guy you like suddenly pushing you against a wall and kissing the heck out of you. As if he can't wait any longer to taste you, to touch you. My whole body's tingling, amplified because at any moment the guard could find us.

Despite being thoroughly sexed up last night and this morning, my body's acting as if we've been separated for-EV-er. My panties are already damp as the hard ridge of his jeans-clad penis rubs against the seam of my pants, which… yeah, wow, that seam rubs me in *the* perfect spot. A sweet ache builds.

The longer we're here, the greater the chance we'll be discovered, but for some reason I can't wait until later. So then, lickety-split it is.

He smoothes his hand up my side and over a breast, and I gasp. "Please tell me you have a condom."

His hand freezes. He steps back so fast, my legs slip down, and I slump against the wall. His hooded gaze pierces mine, and for a flicker of a moment, there's an expression there in his eyes besides lust that I can't quite catch—it went by too fast. Vulnerability?

He reaches into his back pocket, making the scrumptious

muscles of his biceps bunch under his dark red T-shirt.

I'm unbuttoning the top of my Capris and have just managed to shove them and my panties partway down my thighs when he strokes a blunt finger through my folds. He groans. "You're wet, thank fuck."

Then I'm again pushed up the wall, and his tongue, his lips, hot and greedy, plunder my mouth. My legs are constricted by my pants, so I can't wrap them around his waist, but he has his jeans unbuttoned, his boxers shoved out of the way, and a condom on. Dang, this man is fast.

He breaks our fevered kisses and looks at me, his eyes… anguished? "Jane," he rasps.

My legs are thrashing in anticipation, but before I can react further, he wraps his strong arms around my back, captures my mouth in a bruising kiss, and thrusts into me.

Oh holy wow, what a sweet, full ache. *That* was a stroke of possession.

Our tongues tangle and thrust, and he begins moving inside me. It's a different position, with my legs unable to widen, but he does this swivel thing with his hips that grinds him right against my pubic bone. A tight pressure builds and builds. It's almost too much.

Then he eases out and slams into me, hard, possessive. The friction of his retreats and thrusts, the rub of my now-hard nipples against my shirt's fabric mashed to his hard chest, the tangle of our tongues, the gasps of our breaths—it feels as if sensations are building up from points all over me and rushing down to where we're joined.

My orgasm is about on top of me, but it hits me earlier than I expect, and I practically scream into his mouth at the sudden violence of it.

His thrusts grow frantic, less controlled, as if he's no longer worrying about finesse. Vaguely, I'm aware that my thrashing has freed my legs, and even though they feel boneless, somehow I lift them up around his waist. It's almost a relief, instead of having them hang.

"Fuck," he gasps into my mouth.

He lifts me up and away from the wall, so he's gripping my ass. He breaks our kiss, and his mouth latches onto my shoulder. He doesn't bite—it's as if he's finding a way to hold on, hold me to him. His hips are plunging in and out, and we collapse back against the wall. He sinks inside me again and shouts into my shoulder.

Deep inside me, he jerks and pulses, which triggers another searing orgasm.

Holy shit.

As our breaths saw in and out in the hushed quiet of all this nature, hearts pounding against each other like mad, a realization pierces me so hard I'd have doubled over if I wasn't flush against Aiden.

I'm going to have a hard time letting him go.

But I have to. This is just a fling.

A hot fling, but a fling just the same.

I mean, how do I even know if what we shared—all three times—was truly special if I don't have much to compare it to? So far—let's be frank here—so far, I've had pre-Aiden sex ranging across a broad spectrum from shitty to okay. So then how do you judge? Am I just having good sex with a competent lover? Or something more? I could be thinking it's the greatest thing since sliced bread, and he's looking at it going, meh, more sliced bread. Next!

It's these kinds of thoughts that spin around in my head as we quickly dress and start walking back. So much so, that even *I'm* sick of myself.

Oddly, I'm envious of his experience. Because he can accurately *judge*.

AIDEN

Several hours later, Jane parks the car at a rest stop. We found the human sundial on our walk back to the car, but we're a bit behind schedule now, what with the car trouble and the hot-as-fuck sex at the gardens, so we picked up a late lunch in a drive-thru. We stroll in silence to the stone picnic tables in the nearest shade.

Ever since leaving the gardens, Jane's cloaked herself in a new quality of silence. We're still friendly and all, but the air between us hums a bit differently.

Part of it is me, because I'm freaking the shit out.

I like Jane. A lot.

And as my mind used to do with Brittany, it's filled with thoughts of Jane. What she smells like. The timbre of her voice. What she might say to this or that.

Everything in me has subtly shifted to orient toward her.

Again, I'm losing myself in someone else's life. Their needs. Their plans. Hence my mild freak-out—I'm setting myself up for getting hurt.

I've been down this road before. I know how it goes. If I allow it, I'll lose myself in Jane, like I did Brittany. Bend over backward for her. I paid for Brittany's fucking grad school—that's how much of a putz I was. And just when she was set to graduate, and we were to get married, she dumps me. Like I'd been a ghost in *her* life too.

These freak-out thoughts are weighting down the silence as Jane and I make quick work of our lunch so we can hit the road. However, when we return to the car, it won't start. Won't take a jump either.

And we're in the middle of northern Florida.

17

Aiden

After some calls, we find a tow service to haul her car to the nearest garage.

By the time the tow truck driver has her car cranked tight onto the back of his flatbed, it's dusk.

I walk with him back to the cab of his truck, pocketing the card he gave me. "What's the closest decent hotel from here that won't be too far from the garage?"

He scratches his cheek, looking off into the distance. He's wearing a trucker cap with the words "Honk if you see parts fall off."

"There's a decent one near Macclenny," he answers. "It's on the way to the garage." He looks back at me and points with his thumb behind him. "I can give you a ride, if you'd like."

"Thanks, man. That'd be awesome."

After telling Jane about the hotel, I help her throw our gear into the cab and climb in first so she's not next to the guy. He seems nice enough, but I don't want her to feel uncomfortable sandwiched between two large men.

As we head west along the highway and the interstate lights alternately light up and fade out the cab's interior, I have a feeling our little road trip has been permanently derailed.

And though I was just chastising myself for getting in too deep with Jane, I can't abandon her. Nor am I happy about the derailment.

Jane

I collapse onto one of the double beds with a sigh. We're in a moderately priced motel near Macclenny, Florida. We're grumpy and tired, but we're trying to stay positive. I know he has to be worried about how he's going to get to Atlanta now.

I know I am. Worry has settled in my stomach and sits there like a Large Print edition of *War and Peace*.

My phone rings. "Please be the mechanic." I dive for it. "This is Jane."

"Hi, Miss Jane. It's Scott."

I bounce off the bed and start pacing. "Hi. Were you able to determine anything?"

"Yep. Even though I already sent my men home, I took a look for you. It's your alternator."

My stomach dips. "How much?"

"With parts and labor, you're looking at about $550."

A quick mental inventory of my checking and savings account shows that no matter how I shuffle it around, I don't have it. And I don't do credit cards. Shit.

I turn my back to Aiden and lower my voice. "Um, I'll have to get back to you on that."

"Take your time, Miss Jane. We can't start on it until Monday anyway. We're booked solid tomorrow and Saturday, and we're closed on Sunday. We'll keep your car safe here until you get back to us next week."

I squeak out a "thank you" and hang up.

We're screwed.

It's my car and my trip, so there's no way I can ask Aiden for help with the repair money. That's not something you ask of a fling.

Claire. She might spot me. But that still doesn't help the timeline.

I toss my phone onto the bed and face Aiden. "Bad news."

He lays back on the double bed by the door and clasps his hands behind his head. I ignore—*mostly*—what that does to his T-shirt and muscles. The movement exposes a strip of skin above his jeans, complete with happy trail.

I'm sore from all of our sexing, but my lower parts flutter anyway. What the hell? I should be too tired for this. Plus, you know, the timing? Not so great.

"What'd he say?"

I plop on the other bed and tuck my legs up to my chest, arms wrapped tight around them.

I knew this time with Aiden was a fantasy. And reality just invaded. "It'll be $550, but they can't even start until Monday." I prop my chin on a knee.

He drags his hands across his face and thumps his head back against the pillow. The aged A/C under the window does a cough-rattle and kicks in, filling the small room with its hum and cool air.

Time to rip off the Band-Aid and cut loose before I get more sucked in with someone who'll just let me down. Charmers always do. At least with people like me. I don't have the stickiness needed to keep someone smooth like him. Like my mom must have. And I can*not* appear as if I expected more out of what was going on between us. I knew the score, and I'd look like an idiot expecting more.

I'd rather not have that confirmed, thank you very much.

It's a fling. And I can't rely on a fling.

"I'm sorry, Aiden. I know you need to get to Atlanta."

Aiden

Jane sits there, the small gulf of the double beds between us. I'd like to say that the quality of her silence is new, but it's not.

It's the same goddamn coldness I felt the morning after we first met, still fully clothed, but under a pile of blankets.

Jesus, I'm such a fool. Here I thought something was developing between us, something more than just sex. And while, sure, it was freaking me out, I would've dealt.

Bitterness coats my tongue and gut. I've gotta face reality—I'm just a good fuck. Of course someone like Jane wouldn't be into someone like me once we're back in Sarasota. This is a fucking Brittany situation all over again. Except this time, I won't make the mistake of being clueless.

"I need to call Conor," I say into the silence.

She nods, her chin rubbing her knee. "You do what you need to do." Her voice is impersonal, and her eyes have this strange flatness, as if she's erected a wall the size of Fort Knox around her and can't see through it.

I frown. Jesus. I'm not even worth discussing any of this with. I'm not worth even being asked to help. A ghost.

But I can't just abandon her.

Annoyance making my movements jerkier than I'd like, I grab the dinky ice bucket and march down to the ice machine. Once I'm far enough away, I call Conor and give him the scoop.

Surprise, surprise. He's not happy.

I plunk the ice bucket on top of the ice machine and pace the perimeter of the snack alcove. "Yeah, man, I know. Promise. I'll be there in time for the game. I'll find a bus or a car rental or something." I don't know how that's going to work. We're in the middle of nowhere.

But I'm convincing enough that I can hang up with Conor and call the mechanic.

It takes some prodding, but the guy gives a quote for

how much it'll cost to pay someone overtime to come in tomorrow.

"Do it. I'll pay the bill," I tell him. It'll leave me only a couple hundred on my credit card, but it's worth it. Now she won't be stuck here the whole weekend, worrying about her car. This works out great, because even if I can't abandon her, the reality is, I *do* need to get to Atlanta tomorrow. After giving him my card info, I hang up.

Satisfaction warms me that I'm able to do this for her. Take care of her.

And then I grip my hair and pull. Hard.

Shit.

I'm doing it again. I'm becoming a fucking doormat.

I swipe my debit card for a Coke Zero for Jane and a Coke for me and fill up the ice bucket.

I stomp back down the hallway. Fixing her car was necessary. I just need to set boundaries.

I'm horrible with boundaries, but I've gotta start somewhere.

First step, spinning this in a non-doormat way.

I have my game face on when I enter the room. She twists around, her cell to her ear. "Uh-huh. Yes. That works. Thank you," she says and hangs up.

I place the drinks on the bureau. "Okay, so I've been thinking. I talked to Conor, and of course he's not happy."

I wince as I hear how that comes out.

Okay, do this without sounding like a dick. I make sure my voice is more casual than I feel. "I need to get to Atlanta by Saturday. Your car is in the shop until at least Monday. The way I see it, we don't have a lot of options."

Non-doormat groundwork laid. Now to the solution.

But before I can open my mouth to continue, she crosses her arms and says, "I agree." She nods to her cell. "That was a rental car agency. They can drop a car off tonight, and as long as you have a major credit card and your driver's license, you can drive to Atlanta for $89."

What's that odd feeling? Oh, yeah. What it feels like

when someone impales me on a WTF spike.

I'm staring at this woman, whom I thought I might be able to have a relationship with, and she wants nothing more to do with me. She's all but pushing me out the door.

If I wanted a clear signal about where we stand, I got it. "So that's it?"

She sits all prim and proper on the edge of the bed, and I want to push her against the mattress, grip my hands in her hair, and fuck her brains out.

But apparently I'm the only horny bastard in this room. And the only one with any emotional skin in the game.

She looks away. "We both knew this was going to end when we got to Atlanta."

We did?

I don't say anything.

She seems to steel herself. She nods. "It's better this way. Like you said, you need to get to Atlanta. And I know they really want you there tomorrow, not Saturday. Now you can get there in time to bond with the team."

I swallow down my hurt. "This is what you want?"

"This is what I want."

18

JANE

"CRAP."

I punch the remote control button again. "That's crap."

I'm flipping channels trying to find something on the motel TV that isn't a rom-com or a reality show. I've had a bit too much reality for the night.

Aiden left ten minutes ago, and I'm nibbling the last slice of pizza we ordered.

But it tastes like crap. Not even my new jammies are cheering me up—a library due date tank and panty set.

I'm unreasonably upset about this whole mess. I *knew* it was a fling, but somehow I'd let myself get sucked into his charm. I forgot myself during the last two days with him.

While it stung to see him leave me and hop in his rental, it was also a good thing. If I'm already this much sucked in by him after a couple of days, how much harder would it have been when I left him *Saturday?*

Because, yeah, if we'd continued on, I would've stuck around to see his first game before heading back home. I was already starting to build castles in the air. Starting to believe there was something more.

That I'm *this* upset is a wake-up call. And just in time.

I take another bite of pizza.

This is why I prefer to be alone. No nasty plummets from the dizzy heights of expectation.

"Suck it up, buttercup," I mutter and punch the channel changer again.

Aiden

I'm driving west on I-10, leaving Macclenny behind me and telling myself leaving Jane was the smart thing to do.

That I'm respecting her wishes.

That it's time I stopped playing in this stupid bubble we created and get my ass to Atlanta like I'm supposed to.

I take another pull from my now warm Coke, needing the caffeine. I just have to make it to Lake City. I booked a room there, because it's far enough from Jane that I can't act on my wuss instincts and turn around.

My headlights sweep across a hand-painted sign promising juicy citrus. *U-Pick, U-Bag, $7.*

If I'd been driving with Jane and it was daytime, I'd tease her about stopping. She'd protest but not really mean it. We'd examine each pick before putting it in our bag, and I'd try to steal a kiss next to her ear.

Jesus. I'm already a goner.

I'm *not* in a car with Jane. It's *not* daytime. And we're not in some fucking sappy romantic movie.

Yeah, it's a good thing I'm leaving now.

Jane

My motel doesn't have continental breakfast, so I'm scuffling across the deserted road to a diner recommended by the manager. The parking lot pavement's so old, grass pokes up through the radiating cracks.

I'm trying not to feel sorry for myself.

After all, I have my wish now, right? Three whole days where I can veg—by *myself*—and read.

Damn straight. I grip my tablet tighter and push through the door plastered with paper flyers for local events, some out-of-date. The little bell rings, and a few heads blink up at me with bleary eyes before returning to their papers or smart phones.

I select a booth in the back corner and slide across the vinyl seat where a strip of duct tape covers a broken seam. I try to hold on to that resolve when really I'm afraid the ache isn't just the absence of a recent familiarity, but because I've grown feelings for the charmer. Honestly, it feels like I have that string Jane Eyre mentions, tied from my left rib to his.

"What'll ya have, miss?"

A girl about my age looking as if she's about to pop out a baby, she's so huge, holds an order pad, her other arm resting on her preggo belly.

I scan the menu. "Hot tea, and I'll take the breakfast special with the eggs over easy."

"Coming right up." She scoots back to the kitchen area with surprising speed.

I wake up my tablet. The last book I was reading pops up on the page last read. I stare at it.

Aaaand, wow, my mind's scrambling for what the hell I'm even reading. Because it's been that long since I cracked this open. Whoa. Normally, I read every day, and I'm taken aback to realize I haven't read anything in several days. Last night I didn't even pick it up and instead turned on the TV.

I flip back a page and start reading to refresh my memory,

and it doesn't take me long to get back into Loretta Chases's *Mr. Impossible*.

My breakfast soon arrives, but I'm experiencing the hot lashes of a sandstorm as the lovable rogue Rupert protects the brainiac Daphne. Once I finish my breakfast, though, I reluctantly push away my plate and tablet and top off my hot tea. I need to figure out what I'm going to do.

I look at the time on my phone. Almost late enough on a Friday morning for me to call Claire and beg for a loan. Which, man, I hope she can do, because I don't have a lot of options.

I decide to be optimistic and assume she'll come through and I can have my car fixed by Monday. That leaves one more decision—go straight home or continue the trip?

I need to call the library and ask for Monday off anyway, since I can't leave until then. So do I also ask for Tuesday off and finish Claire's route or hightail it home once my car's fixed?

From the corner of my eyes, I see my tablet fade to black from inactivity, dousing the words I just left. When I was caught up in their tale. Oddly, a pang of longing pierces me. A longing for more. Yeah, I'm enjoying their story, but I'm reading about someone *else's* life. And while there's no way I'll give that up, can't I have both?

And then a new feeling suffuses me, one that makes me choke up as well as flip the contents of my belly from excitement.

Yes. Yes, I can. I'm going to finish the trip. And not just because I want Claire to reconcile with her mom, though she'd probably concede that my car failure constitutes an exception.

I want to finish for *me*.

Aiden

I toss the empty can of Red Bull onto the floor of the rental and follow the directions Google calls out for the team's hotel in Atlanta.

I'd like to say I had a lovely, refreshing eight hours of sleep at a luxurious hotel last night, but my nose would grow so long, it'd punch through the windshield.

Can't have that.

Especially since it's a rental.

Jesus, I'm getting punch-drunk.

I pull into the parking lot and navigate to a shady spot. I need to get my head on straight before I face the guys, or they'll ferret out something's up and I'll never hear the end of it.

Last night, besides thoughts of Jane, which necessitated rubbing one out in the shower before collapsing into bed *and* again this morning, all of my interactions with Brittany paraded through my mind. I kept trying to shove her out of my mind, where she belongs, but I failed miserably.

Now, for the first time since she left me at the altar, I sift through our time together, looking for where I went wrong. After that disastrous day, I was too devastated to analyze it all. I think I was too afraid. Too hurt.

I wanted to forget her. Thoroughly. Hence losing myself in mindless hookups.

The problem is, I had no closure.

No explanation.

And I was too angry and hurt to demand one, if she'd even have let me ask.

I snag my cell from the passenger seat and do what I'd resisted doing ever since—look Brittany up on Facebook. I'd unfollowed her right after, unwilling to cut the tie completely by unfriending her, but also not wanting to have her life pop up into my feed on a regular basis. No, thank you.

Surprisingly, we're still friends, so I'm able to see her profile.

Seeing her face in a picture that's not familiar to me doesn't cause any ripples whatsoever.

Interesting.

I mean, I knew I was over her, but I thought I'd feel *something*. I scroll through her feed. She hasn't changed a whole lot. There's a plea for signing a petition to save an endangered animal. There's a meme from one of her favorite movies. Vacation pics.

Then I notice that a lot of the vacation pics feature the same guy and the more recent ones have a baby.

Fully aware I'm straight out stalking, I click over to see her relationship status. Married.

On a hunch, I scroll to the time period when *we* were supposed to be married. She graduated on time. Then I see the notice where she's tagged herself as being married. And it's only two fucking months after she left me.

Well, the timing's suspicious but not definitive that she left me for another guy. But it's all the closure I'm going to get.

Closure.

Having that now—man, it shifts something into place inside me. Something I didn't realize was out of whack.

That's all I'd wanted. To know why.

And because I'm a sorry putz, I click into the search box. My finger hovers over the keys.

"Fuck it," I mutter.

I type in Jane's name and find her profile. My gut flips when her profile photo appears. She's at a café table reading a book, and someone's captured her just as her hand raises up to block the shot.

There's a half smile, as if she knows she should be more social with whomever she's with, but she's gotta read a little bit more. From the background, it appears she's at a café on Siesta Key.

Most of her profile is locked down, so there's not much more on her timeline than that photo and public notices for events at the library, but I click to her photos page anyway. To see if she's with any other guys. The thought of even seeing a pic of her with another guy sends an unreasonable flash of jealousy through me. I sit back and toss the cell into the passenger seat.

Fuck.

I have it bad for her.

I've also been an idiot—Jane's nothing like Brittany.

I can't just assume that because she's serious and screams relationship-material I'll lose myself in her and she'll just take-take-take.

I have no idea if she *does* want more from me than sex, but maybe I can convince her there's more to me.

I snatch my cell and look at the screen. Fuck it. I still have time. I shift the car into reverse and pull out of the parking lot.

19

Jane

I punch the pillow behind my head. Get fluffier, dangit.

Can't get *comfortable*. I fall back with a sigh and flip to the next page in my ebook.

I haven't been able to get a hold of Claire yet—she teaches sailing, and summer camp is still going on. I'll have to wait until tonight. I should have woken her up this morning before she set out, but it's not as if I'm in a rush—they can't work on it until Monday anyway.

A knock on the hotel door startles me. What the—?

My heart races as it obviously has stupid hopes that it's Aiden.

"It's not him," I mutter as I scramble off the bed and bolt to the door.

I peek through the peephole. It's the tow truck driver from last night.

My stupid heart crosses its arms in a huff. Frowning, I open the door.

"Hey, Miss Jane." He holds up my keys and shakes them. "You're all set."

I blink, because…what?

I peer past his shoulder. My car's in a patch of shade off to the right.

"How... My car. It's fixed? I thought..."

He gives me a funny look. "Didn't your guy tell you? He paid one of Scott's mechanics overtime so you guys could have your car finished up today."

He... But...

"Wow. Like Mr. Darcy," I whisper. I mean, not with fixing a car, obviously. But fixing a problem of mine without telling me.

"Ma'am?"

I shake my head never mind. Dazed, somehow I manage to hold out my hand for the keys and thank him.

I let the door fall shut and shuffle over to the bed as confusion clouds my mind.

Why didn't Aiden tell me?

He came in from outside after we first arrived, where he clearly made some calls as well as getting ice and Cokes. He told me about how he needed to get to Atlanta, and...

Shit. I cut him off to tell him I had a rental for him.

I was so determined to not let myself get attached to a charmer—and spare myself a letdown—that I pretty much pushed him out the door.

Pretty much? There was no *pretty much* about it. I *did* push him away.

My heart perks back up, the sap, pointing an accusatory finger at me—*See? He likes us!*

I point out he was just being practical—we needed the car fixed, and he had a tight timeline.

I fall back against the lumpy pillow and stare at the ceiling. I need psychiatric help, clearly, because I'm anthropomorphizing my heart. Gah!

Okay, if his gesture was pure practicality, why didn't he just tell me and save himself the expense of the rental car on top of the mechanic?

My heart wins this round. I bounce off the bed and start stuffing my scattered belongings into my suitcase.

I'm going to finish this trek now, but instead of turning around and heading back after reaching Atlanta, I'm going to Aiden's game. Because if there's a possibility that Aiden gets me like Rupert understands Daphne, I'm going to risk finding out.

Aiden

Jesus Christ in a Clown Car, my palms are sweating. It's almost four in the afternoon, and I'm pulling into Ashburn, Georgia, for Jane's last stop on her trip.

What's here? Besides her soon (hopefully)?

The World's Largest Peanut, of course.

Before leaving Atlanta, I called the mechanic to get an update, and as requested, he called about an hour ago to say the car was being delivered to Jane.

So, according to Google, she'll arrive in about an hour.

If she decided to continue her trek.

And that's a big fat fucking if.

The kicker? I can't even call her because we never exchanged cell numbers. And Claire sure as hell isn't going to give it to me. So I'm going to camp out as long as the site will allow.

The giant peanut on a brick tower is visible from I-75, but when I pull off the interstate, I can't find the stupid road that'll get me there. No signs point the way, so I keep trying side roads. After a turnaround in an apartment complex, I find the right road.

I'm trying not to see this as a fucking metaphor for my love life.

The giant peanut looms at the end of a stretch of road surrounded by empty fields and patches of pine trees and shrubs, with the interstate as backdrop.

I park in front of it, the only car here. Conveniently,

there's a gazebo housing a picnic table where I can wait for as long as I'm able before I have to make the two-plus hour trek back to Atlanta.

If she doesn't show before then? Well, then time for Plan B, whatever that will be. Looks as if I'll have time to figure that out.

The gazebo and picnic table give me an idea, though.

Jane

Up ahead, the giant peanut beckons in solitary glory from the side of the interstate. It's been an uneventful two-hour drive, but I don't use the time to listen to an audiobook like I'd normally do on a road trip.

Instead, I stew in my thoughts. A strange mixture churns inside me, and I need the time to separate my thoughts out.

Part of me is miserable at how things ended with Aiden and how I so quickly wrote him off. There's guilt there too, that he went to so much trouble and I didn't even know it until the keys showed up today with my car.

Yeah, I feel like a total bitch, okay?

Part of me is also excited about seeing a stupid giant peanut, and I owe a lot of this excitement to Aiden. He helped me become more engaged with these crazy-wacky sites. Helped me see them as something worth noticing and experiencing. As if this engagement was an unused muscle before and he helped creak it into use, and now I can't stop.

Which also makes me wish that he could be at this last site with me. But that's tonight.

Tonight, I'll be in Atlanta and can try to make amends. I have no idea if any of what I'm feeling is just me, but I need to find out. I'm going to dare to climb that height of expectation. After I packed and left the motel, I texted Claire for the team's hotel info.

She called back later, wanting to know what the emergency had been earlier, and I filled her in on the car trouble. Thank God she couldn't talk long because she was rushing to make her flight for Atlanta—she's coming up tonight with the women's team—otherwise she'd have grilled me more. I also thanked her for the trip. At first she thought I was being sarcastic, considering my car just broke down. But I was serious. She was right. I needed this journey.

Time to my thoughts also let another nugget float to the top: slipping and making a literary reference with the tow truck driver earlier when I was flustered made me realize I haven't done that in a while. Which led me to wonder—why?

My conclusion? And this threw me. In those moments, I think I wasn't quite fitting into the world. It was my way of processing and relating my experiences to what I *did* know. And lately with Aiden, I was experiencing the world in a more…involved way? On my own terms?

Something like that, anyway.

Miss Google speaks up, and I exit onto the off ramp and follow her instructions. I didn't *quite* break our rule about looking up our sites, but I also didn't want to waste time searching for the site, so I went on roadsideamerica.com and found the exact GPS coordinates.

A couple of turns later, and the monument to the peanut is straight ahead at the end of the road.

Damn. Another car's there. I won't have it to myself.

And then I catch myself.

No.

That was the old me.

The new me should embrace interacting with others.

I park next to the other car and grab my Polaroid and journal. Someone inside the gazebo stands.

Hmm. Maybe this isn't such a great idea as they look to be man-shaped and there's no one else nearby.

I'll just make this quick.

I step out, not making eye contact, and edge around the giant peanut so I can get a Polaroid for my journal.

The film pops out. As I lower the camera, my gaze brushes past the gazebo, and my heart friggin' stops.

It's Aiden, leaning against a support post for the gazebo.

I take a couple of steps forward, and jeez, my legs are a little shaky. "You're here."

He's mostly in shadow, but I can see his big grin, which sets loose not only a swarm of butterflies in my stomach, but a twinge of heat in my lady parts.

As I approach, though, I notice his leg's bent back, and he's tapping his toe against the decking.

His hands are in his front pockets, and the way he's leaning against the post is pure hunk, highlighting his height and his muscles. But that tap-tap-tap?

Holy crap. He's *nervous*.

Right then and there, my heart drops out of my chest and melts at my feet. Especially when I see behind him a picnic table loaded with food, two wine glasses, and a bottle of wine.

20

Aiden

I have the casual lean going as Jane approaches, the sun behind her purpling the clouds as it descends.

But inside I'm all kinds of emotional. It's killing me not to close the distance between us and gather her against me. Seeing her exit the car—fuck—it was like fireworks exploded and I was motionless from the shock of it.

I mean, I know I'm attracted to her like no one else, but this was…different. It was relief and contentment and *rightness*. As if everything around me was back in its place.

But, Jesus, I have no idea if she feels the same.

I've never risked this kind of leap before.

Not even with Brittany. That sounds weird, I know, because we were engaged, but getting married was just talked about as a given. There was no palm-sweating, heart-pounding scene as I whipped out a ring or anything.

Now, though?

Palms sweating—check.

Heart pounding—check.

When I saw the gazebo, I dashed to a nearby package store and bought wine. Foraged for the picnic set up behind me. But it's more than food laid out on that table. It's everything inside me too. There for her to see. Jesus, I feel exposed. No passing this off with a quip if it all goes south.

The doubt and the nerves that plagued me as I shopped were a fucking wake-up call. I agonized over the wine and took items in and out of my shopping cart, wondering if she liked them or not. Or if they were stupid.

I never had this kind of doubt with Brittany. We'd been a couple all through college, then through her grad school, and it was a natural step to get married. So it seemed to me.

I never questioned it.

As I mentally slapped myself at the local mart and went with my gut on the food, it hit me—Brittany did me a favor. It was shitty of her to not be upfront about her feelings—*and* still take my tuition payments—but yeah. We weren't meant to be together.

I have no idea if Jane and I are either, but I want to find out.

Now she's here, peering past me at the picnic I've laid out. Her eyes widen. I tense.

She swallows and looks back at me, her eyes soft. A burst of hope arcs through me.

She smiles. "Oh good. I'm hungry."

I laugh, and the awkward tension rarely between us dissipates.

"Took you long enough." I nod toward the object looming behind her. "Like the giant peanut?"

She glances back, her face relaxed. "It's, well, *big*, that's for sure."

"Got some smaller nuts inside. Come on in."

She raises a brow and looks at my crotch.

"You wound me. Seriously, I do have some peanuts. Boiled and roasted. Figured it was required for a picnic here."

Her tension-easing teasing *could* be to help me save face, letting me know she only sees me as a source of good sex, but I'm hoping not.

Only one way to find out.

She brushes past me, her scent faint but taunting me all the same. She settles onto a bench, and I take the seat opposite and pour wine into our glasses.

I lift mine in a toast. "To the quirkiness of humankind."

She lifts hers and gives me a full smile. "Cheers to that."

We click glasses and take a sip. She sets her glass down. "What have we got here?"

I wave a hand across the spread. "Cheese, chicken salad, peanuts, and a pecan log, because that also seemed appropriate."

"Pecan logs! I haven't had one since I was a kid. We used to take summer vacations up the coast, and we'd stop at Stuckey's when we came through Georgia." Outwardly, her voice is excited, but there's a quality to it and her movements which belie her nervousness. She's using the picnic as cover. This could be good or bad.

I slice off a piece of the weird concoction and nudge it onto a plate for her. Honestly, I have no idea what that stuff's made of. She slices some of the cheese and makes a mini-heap of boiled peanuts.

Not the classiest picnic, but my time and the local resources were limited.

But now that it's time for me to talk, I hesitate. Fuck, I'm such a wuss. I'm marshalling my thoughts, ready to lay out my arguments, when Jane clears her throat.

"Aiden…"

My stomach drops—her voice now has a tentative quality like she's about to step in a minefield. Here it comes. Fuck. I *am* a fool.

She fiddles with the slice of cheese, getting it lined up just right on her cracker. "I…I want to apologize for how I acted last night. I let my insecurities and hang-ups rule me. Not proud of it, but I want you to know I regret how I handled it. I shouldn't have shut down and pushed you away like that. You didn't deserve it. And…" She takes a deep breath. "And thank you for getting my car fixed. I know you did it because you needed to get here, but I—"

Here goes nothing.

I reach across and take her hand, but I can't look at her

face. Not yet.

Jesus, I had no idea I was such a chickenshit. "Hold up. I know I laid it on thick last night to make it seem like it, but that's not the reason."

"No?" Her whispered question floats down to my ear.

I glance up. "You're not the only one caught up in a weird headspace. That was me trying to save face. Because my main motivation was all you. I wanted to do that for you. I wanted to help you. But when you shut me out after the call with the mechanic, I panicked. I marched into that room to make it sound like I was doing it all for me. So instead of telling you my plans right away, I laid the groundwork by saying how important it was for *me* to get to Atlanta."

"And then I hit you with the rental car before you had the chance."

I take a sip of wine. "Yep."

"Aiden, what's going on here?"

I could play dumb, but I'm not going to insult her by misunderstanding. "I'm not sure."

"You're not sure?" She tugs on her hand, slipping it from under mine.

I catch her hand in time and grip it tight. There's a slight flush in her cheeks, and her eyes are wide. She looks so vulnerable, I just want to pull her into a big hug.

Jesus. This hugging urge is weird.

But there it is.

"That didn't come out right," I say.

She waits in her quiet space, and I hope to God I can find the right words so I can be in that space alongside her.

Because that's where I want to be more than anyplace else in the world.

"I need to back up." I rub a thumb across her smooth skin. Back and forth. Back and forth. "Do you know I haven't been able to stop thinking about you since we had that impromptu movie marathon?"

I watch her face intently, soaking up any little clue as to her headspace.

"You haven't?" she asks in a small voice, but there's a trace of disbelief in it.

I hold her gaze. "No. I…I had a great time that night, and when you blew me off the next morning…"

A shield slams down over her gaze, and despite the fact that I'm holding her hand, that shield feels like it's between us in the air too. "You saw me as a challenge. One of the few women who resisted you."

My jaw clenches. "That's not it at all. I was puzzled, yes—"

She scoffs at that.

"Not because I have such a huge ego that I expected you to fall at my feet. It's because we just…clicked that night, and I really enjoyed hanging out with you. I thought the feeling was mutual. I was a bit freaked out by that feeling, honest to God, but it was there."

She's holding my gaze so intently, it's as if she's scared that if she looks away, I'll disappear. "We *did* click."

"Then what happened?"

She stares at me for a full minute. And there it is again. That quality to her quietness where she's on the cusp of taking a risk and screwing up the nerve.

Hope doesn't spark inside only to sputter out. Now it lights me up with enough strength to burn steady.

"I was so giddy about meeting you," she says in a rush of breath, "and how much fun we had, and that we'd fallen asleep together, and you didn't try anything, that I had to text my best friend with the news. I just couldn't believe that such a…" She blushes again. "Such a hot guy was into me and was also respectful enough to not push anything sex-wise."

Coldness washes through me, banking that hopeful glow a bit, because I can guess what happened. "Claire."

She nods. "Claire. She wanted to know who the lucky guy was. She'd left the party early because she and Conor had some kind of tiff." Here her eyes go big again, and she claps a hand over her mouth.

Her words confirm a suspicion I've had, but I shake my head and say, "Those two kids."

She laughs. "Yeah. So, anyway…" She takes a deep breath. "Claire freaked out when she heard it was you."

I thread my fingers through hers and look at our joined hands, grateful that I'm at least still holding them. "Lemme guess. She regaled you with my past. Called me a man-whore." That last part wasn't a guess—Claire has called me that to my face before. Multiple times.

"Yes."

I frown and glance back up at her. "But didn't the fact that I *didn't* try anything tell you something?"

She darts her gaze away and won't meet my eyes. "Jane?"

I rub her hand again, and a surge of triumph pulses through me when I can feel her tremor slightly at my touch. Then I call myself an idiot, because chemistry between us has never been in doubt.

She studies our clasped hands, and her voice is so faint I have to lean forward to hear. "…that you weren't, er, interested in me that way."

I jump off the seat and scramble around to her side, sitting beside her. That table was becoming a fucking metaphor for what's between us. "Wait. Back up." I only caught the tail end of her sentence, but it was enough to make my stomach drop to my feet. "You thought I made no moves on you because I wasn't interested?"

"Yeah."

"Explain this to me."

"I, um, well, when Claire said you were a player, that you basically plowed through women, I…I, well, at first I was disappointed. And then I was hurt. Because if you were such a player, and you…"

She trails off, and I cup her cheek and smooth a finger along her temple. "And I…?"

She appears to gather herself. "I assumed it was because you weren't attracted to me that way. That if I couldn't even get a player, um, worked up…"

I think my heart kind of squeezes in sympathy at that.

"Jesus. Are you serious?"

She flinches, and I curse at myself. I grasp both sides of her face so I can keep her gaze on me. "I wanted you so bad that night, but something held me back."

That shadow of insecurity clouds her gaze again.

"Stop that." I stroke my thumbs across her cheekbones. "I'm not sure what stopped me that night, but it wasn't lack of interest, I'll tell you that. Jesus Christ, our chemistry was off the charts. You had to have felt that. But…" And I need to be completely honest here—with her and myself. "I don't think I was ready then for something more than a fling. I needed a chance to sort that out in my head, but I also knew once we got together, it'd be explosive, and I wanted to hold off."

"So you *did* want to rip my clothes off that night?" The woman who I've come to know in bed, with her newfound sexual confidence, peeks through, lending a tease to her voice.

I breathe out. "Fuck yeah."

There's more that needs to be said, so for now I lean over and brush her lips with mine instead of doing what my body aches to do—lay her beneath me on this damn table. Or bending her over it would work too. Or just kissing the shit out of her.

I sit back and pick up my wine glass, and she does the same. Already the quality of the air has shifted. From wary nervousness to anticipation. "I should've sought you out after. You ghosting me was for the best, I figured. I *was* a man-whore, and thought that was how it should be with me. But when you showed up that afternoon at my bar, then the gas station, and I had the opportunity to hang out with you for several days? Yeah, I jumped on it."

At that, she flushes, but she also looks a tad guilty. I cock my head in question.

"Um. I need to confess something," she says.

"Okay." I wave to the roof over our heads. "You know this is the Gazebo of Confession. You have to lay it all out there."

She laughs. "The Gazebo of Confession, huh? Next to

the giant peanut?"

"Yep. It's in the guidebook." She looks doubtful, and rightly so. "Peanuts are a legume. Which…rhymes with assume. And you know what happens when you assume. So confessions are a natural consequence."

Like I hoped, she laughs. "That's a bit of a stretch."

"How about this." I rub my jaw, thinking. "The nickname for a peanut is goober, right?"

"Yeah."

"So when you confess, you feel like a complete goober."

She gives a cute snort. "God, you're such a dork." But she says this as if it's the greatest compliment, and it makes me ridiculously happy.

I do a mock bow, but she's not finished.

"And why would I want to look like a goober in front of you?"

"Because I'm one too? So you're safe being a goober with me? Trust me, I'll come out looking like the gooberiest. I have more confessions too."

And this is one of the reasons I'm crazy about Jane. She takes this as straight as can be. Her face goes serious. "I only told you part of the truth. This trip? It wasn't only about me needing to break out of my shell, as Claire termed it."

"Go on." Because I can tell this is hard for her, I take her hand again.

"It was also to purge you from my thoughts."

Internally I do a fuck-yeah fist pump. Which, I know, doesn't make any sense, but at least I was in her thoughts that deeply, right? Which means there's a chance…

She continues, "So Claire had this trip planned, and I was supposed to kick it off by, um, doing something symbolic at your bar."

I frown and run our interaction in the parking lot through my mind. "The fire."

She nods.

"What did you burn, young lady?" I say in a mock-stern voice.

But then I regret teasing her, because she's now red all over and keeps opening and closing her mouth. I pull her hand forward. "You can tell me."

She swallows. "A dil—" and the rest is swallowed in a mumble.

"A what?"

She straightens. "A dildo!" She shouts it and darts her gaze around. And then she bursts out laughing. "A red dildo. I burned a dildo in effigy in your parking lot."

My dick, honest to God, retracts a smidge. "A dildo? You burned a dildo in a symbolic act to purge me from your thoughts?"

"Yes." And then her eyes shine with glee. "And then you stepped in it to put out the last of the flames." She starts to laugh again, and fuck, I love her laugh. It feels free.

"I did step in it, didn't I?" I smile. "Well, that's certainly a way to kick off a road trip."

21

Jane

I SIP THE wine and nibble on the cheese as if I'm all calm, but inside me, everything's a discordant jangle of nerves—happiness, relief, disbelief.

Because...because it looks as if this hot-as-sin man sitting next to me is also a sweet, dorky guy who is actually, possibly interested in me.

And I've misjudged him unfairly. Let Claire's judgment cloud mine. Let my past experience color how I viewed him.

But there's something he said earlier that I'd mentally bookmarked to circle back to.

"You said you were in a weird headspace last night too? An old habit you fell into?"

He rubs his jaw. "Yeah. So. Gazebo Confession time. I was engaged once."

"You?" When he flinches, I realize how that sounded. "I'm sorry." Jeez. I'm *still* misjudging him.

"No." He rubs a hand down his face and blows out a breath. "It's understandable. I haven't exactly been the poster child for steady relationships." He crosses his arms on top of the table and leans forward. "Okay. So. Her name was Brittany, and we met in college. I came from a family whose parents were still married and loved each other. Still do. So it seemed like a natural thing to put everything into the first serious relationship I found myself in."

"Found yourself in?"

He gives a puzzled smile and looks at me, his chin on his shoulder. "Yeah. I just realized how I phrased that. But…" He gazes past me. "It fits. I think since I found it natural to be in a serious relationship, I didn't question it. Didn't stop to wonder if Brittany was right for me."

He returns to staring straight ahead, which puts him in profile. "We got along, and after college, I proposed. She didn't quite turn me down. She wanted to work through grad school first. Always had a dream of getting her master's in education. But she couldn't afford it, so she needed to work her ass off for the tuition, which meant keeping her course load light. Said she wanted to get married, but only after she earned her degree. I figured we're getting married eventually, so why not make it happen sooner. I paid the balance of her tuition not covered by grants. I was making good money in the tech industry and had stock options I could cash out."

A sick feeling churns my stomach. Mixed with anger on his behalf. "What happened?"

He straddles the bench to face me and leans forward, propping himself on his hands, making his arms into an upside-down triangle. I…I only admire what that does to his arm muscles for two seconds. And feel ashamed for even those two seconds amidst his confession.

His smile's resigned, with a bit of what-can-ya-do. "I paid her way through. And we set a wedding date for right before her graduation. And, well, she left me standing at the altar."

I gasp. I had expected something bad to have happened, obviously, but that confession floors me. I stare at the man whom I'd taken for a player—to learn he used to be Mr. Commitment makes me shuffle some assumptions out of the way. "So…the whole ladies-man persona…"

"Was how I coped. It was stupid, but then again, I *am* a guy in my twenties." He flicks the side of his head. "Not much emotional intelligence up here."

"I think you have more than you realize."

He gives me a sad smile. "Maybe…"

"You do, Aiden, trust me, okay?"

He nods, but I can tell he's explained all he cares to right now and is ready to move on. I dig into the cheese and the boiled peanuts, because our time's running out here—the sun's setting and the mosquitoes will be out soon.

"My turn," I say. "The Gazebo of Confession compels me." I push-squirt a boiled peanut into my mouth.

He takes a sip of wine. "Hit me."

"I had a serious relationship right out of college too. Did the whole living together thing. I even kept my job search narrowed to the city where we lived to make staying together easier."

He was a charmer too. Knew how to make me laugh. Like Aiden.

No, not like Aiden. Brett would *never* have had an adult conversation like this.

"What did the fucker do?"

I laugh, and somehow it makes it easier to spill. "One night, I was working a double at my waitressing job. It was a common occurrence. I was picking up as many shifts as I could to save up money. But that night it was unusually slow, and I was the first cut. Even though I needed the money, I was excited to get home because Brett and I could finish our *Arrested Development* binge-watch. I stopped on the way home and picked up his favorite beer and snack food. When I arrived at our apartment, he wasn't hanging out on the couch or in the kitchen. His car was outside, so I knew he was home, but I figured he must be taking a nap, so I queued up a different show I was binge-watching on my own."

I take a deep breath. "I was respecting his privacy, you know? That was one thing he was great about—we could do our own thing even when we were living in the same space. Anyway, I settled on the couch, with my cushions just right, when I heard a thump."

Embarrassment washes through me. God, I can't believe I'm about to tell him all this. I continue before I can think better of it. "I thought maybe he woke up and tripped, so I stopped the movie in case he came out." I clear my throat. "And then I heard another thump. And another. And another."

I give a thready laugh. "Even then, I didn't get it. It was just so outside of the realm of possibility, you know? I was starting to worry, I don't know, that maybe he was thrashing in his sleep? Some nightmare? So, like an idiot, I went down the hall. I opened the door and heard someone say, 'Fuck. Yeah, Brett. Give it to me good.' And there on *our* bed, he was screwing the downstairs neighbor from behind. They were so into it they didn't even notice me. He's…he's pounding away, and a rage I'd never felt propelled me forward." I stop and stare off into the distance, reliving that horrible, mortifying night.

Warm hands clasp mine, and I look back at Aiden. His eyes are hard, and the muscle in his jaw's ticking. "What an asshole."

"Yeah. And you know what he did? Called *me* a bitch. I mean, yeah, I'd rushed forward and pushed against his shoulder with everything I had so that they toppled to the bed, all tangled up. After they stared at me in confusion, both breathing heavy, for what seemed like forever, I turned away, ready to get out of there. That's when he starts ranting, calling me a bitch, and basically twisting the whole thing into my fault. That I was supposed to be working, and that I was working too much so he had to get it somewhere, et cetera. He was good at shifting anything that reflected negatively on him into my fault. Arguing in a way that would tie me up mentally and verbally. Took a while for me to see that."

"I'm sorry he did that to you. Fucker didn't deserve you."

I smile at that. "Thanks. Yeah. Took me a while to see that too. That it wasn't my fault. I thought I was over him, but now I'm not so sure."

He starts and straightens, placing his hands on his thighs. "You're still in love with that asshole?"

"God no. I just mean that I thought I'd moved past the pain he caused. But looking back, I think I let it color how I view men, and myself, if I'm being honest."

"Because of one guy?"

"Not just him. See, Brett was a charmer. A smooth-talker."

Aiden makes a face and rubs his hands down his thighs and back. "Like me."

I shrug and nod. "And my dad. And, well, when you didn't show any interest in me that night, I think deep down it verified a fear I didn't even realize I had."

"What's that?"

It's telling that I have no trouble confessing all this to him. "That I'm too *off*, too boring, to interest someone like Brett, or you, or even my dad."

"Your *dad?*"

I shrug again. "He just seemed to tolerate me. He talked a big talk, made all these promises to me, but he just… couldn't seem to be bothered to follow through. Stupidly, I saw that situation with Brett as my fault in the beginning. That's how good he was at manipulating me—that it was my fault because I couldn't hold his interest. Turns out he and that neighbor had been carrying on for a good while. Any time I worked nights."

"I'd like to find this Brett and twist his dick off for you."

I laugh, but when he doesn't chuckle, I stop. He's serious. His fingers are gripping his knees so hard the knuckles are white. And it warms me to see this guy who's usually smiling and laughing and keeping everyone entertained so deadly serious.

"Thanks, but I'm sure he's gotten what he deserved. I kicked him out of the apartment, of course, but then all he did was move into that chick's apartment. It wasn't too long after that I saw all his stuff piled in front of the building. I never saw him again. Then I was offered the job here and moved." I shrug, glad to have that all out there, for him to make what he will of it.

I'm tired of hiding.

22

Aiden

Jane and I are about to enter an elevator again, this time in the team's hotel in Atlanta. Unlike how I felt two nights ago in Daytona Beach, I'm not nervous or feeling awkward at the artificial intimacy of spending the night in the same room.

Luckily, Jane booked a room before she left Macclenny, so we're spared having to scramble to find one for ourselves. No way am I not spending tonight with her, and no way are we bunking with Paolo.

Shortly after she told me about what that fucker Brett did, we left the giant peanut because of invading gnats and mosquitoes. I found a branch for the rental agency nearby, and so after I dropped the car off, I jumped into hers and up we came.

Perhaps because we shared a shit ton under that gazebo, we were quiet on the drive. Instead, we listened to an audiobook, and sharing that with her made me feel as if I'd made it inside her quiet space.

I think we also knew that if we even once did anything like kiss or touch, we'd be on each other. And no way did I want our next time to be a desperate, roadside fuck. So we were keeping everything on a low simmer.

But as the elevator doors ding shut, and we're the only

ones inside? It's like a sound of permission, because the next thing I know, I have her delicious body pressed up against the wall, and her legs are gripping my hips. I have no clue which of us initiated. The elevator *dinged*, and here we are, my hips grinding into her while my tongue thrusts inside her.

Her nails scrape against my scalp, and she moans and strokes her tongue across mine. And as always, it's a feedback loop. The more I touch her, the more I smell her, feel her, the more I want her. And the more worked up she gets too.

The elevator dings again, and Pepper's voice says, "Aiden?"

We spring apart so fast my back smacks against the opposite wall. We're both panting, looking at Luke and Pepper as they push onto the elevator and hit the button for their floor, one above ours.

Pepper just looks intrigued. Luke? Storm cloud brewing on that face. "Are you Jane, Claire's friend?" he asks her.

She nods, and Luke whirls on me and points his goddamn finger at me. "I told you to keep it in your goddamn pants."

Anger surges inside me, and I'm about to lay into him. He's my teammate, sure, but he's not my fucking dad.

But before I can say anything, Jane pops away from the wall and pulls on his arm. It does nothing to budge him in any direction, because, well, he's a former Navy SEAL, but Jane's not deterred.

She marches around until she's blocking him from me.

I think my heart just about bursts right then. It's an embarrassing feeling. And I'm glad it's not visible, or Luke'd be taking my man card for sure.

But you know what? I don't fucking care.

The only person I care about what they think of me is standing like a tiny Valkyrie, ready to fight for me.

She points a finger at him. "I don't know who you are, but I didn't ask you to defend me, did I?"

Luke backs up, and I'd laugh at the comical look on his face, but he could take me. Not *easily*, but c'mon. He's a SEAL. I'd go down.

At first, I'm as startled as Luke, but I recover faster. I've been seeing her transformation into her more confident self all along, haven't I? I can see she's trembling though. Not so much that it's obvious to Luke and Pepper, but it is to me. And, Goddamn, I want to scoop her up and whisper, *it's all right*, but I know that's not what she needs.

Jane's not done. She steps forward. Pokes her finger into his chest. "I'm a grown woman, and I can take care of myself."

"Yes, ma'am," he says.

Pepper's got a huge grin on her face. "She's got you there, sweetie." She elbows Luke out of the way and holds out her hand. "I'm Pepper. I think we could be great friends."

Thank-fucking-God our floor finally arrives. I snake an arm around Jane and pull her through as she's saying, "I'd like that."

Pepper says, "You coming to the game tomorrow?"

And Jane answers, "Yep," before the doors finally close on the cock blockers.

"You're coming to the game?"

She smiles and rubs my chest. "Of course I am. Miss a chance to see you run around on a field, doing…whatever sport you do, and getting all sweaty?"

That sounds gross to me, but she says it like it's a turn-on. "It's hurling."

"Can't wait."

I pull her hips to mine. "I'll tell you what I can't wait for."

Her eyes go all big, and she bites her lip. "I can't either," she breathes. Then she grabs my hand, looks at the room signs, and starts hightailing it down the hall, practically dragging me.

I hike my duffel bag onto my shoulder and get a firm grip on her carry-on handle, and soon we're both running to the room.

Jane

We collapse onto the bed, laughing. Our sprint down the hall's left us a little out of breath. Okay, *I'm* a little out of breath. Jeez, I need to exercise more.

As my head hits the soft pillow, Aiden swings a jean-clad leg over my hips, pinning me. Wow. He's a glorious mountain of muscle sitting on top of me, a huge grin across his handsome face. The neon lights offered up by Atlanta's night sky highlight the strong, angular lines of his face and body, even with all his clothes on. His hair's all mussed from our make-out session in the elevator when I couldn't get close enough.

He rubs his hands down his muscular thighs, and his eyes track up and down, stopping first on my lips, then down my neck to my chest, then down my stomach.

Dang, just his gaze grazing my body heats me up everywhere. I push up with my hips. His eyes snap to mine and darken. Holy cow, he looks as if he could just eat me up.

Yes, please.

I do another hip swivel, though my range of motion is pretty much nil due to his weight. He gets the message, though, and grabs the edge of my shirt, his knuckles skimming my stomach and making me shiver from the contact. I lift up, and he whips it off over my head. My shirt is still floating to the ground when his warm, strong hands caress my waist. He brushes his palms up, slowly, so that all my senses have time to gather and then concentrate where he strokes my skin. I arch my chest in invitation, but he skims back down to my waist. Up again, and then back down.

"Aiden!" My voice might have come out sounding a tad needy.

"What, baby?"

"Breasts."

"Yes? They're quite lovely. What about them?" He looks his fill but doesn't stroke his hands higher.

"Your hands. On me. My breasts. Now."

His eyes flare with heat. "You're bossy."

"You love it." I gasp as his fingers skim the sensitized skin just above my bra. I'm awake for him *everywhere.*

"I do," he rumbles.

And I do too. I lever up and grasp the clasp at the back, my fumbling fingers stretching out the unclasping business muuuuch longer than usual. Stupid tiny clasps. Finally, it pops free, and I fling my bra across the room. Just as I settle back against the cool sheets, a wet warmth clamps around one of my nipples and tugs.

"Holy shit." Heat spears from that point and arrows straight down to my clit, flooding me with sensual heat. I clasp his face to hold him there, but he edges away with a slight chuckle. I glance down in time to see his tongue flick my now-hard nipple.

Oh God.

He cups that breast and plumps it up. "God, you have great tits. Did I tell you that?"

"No," I gasp as he feathers a kiss across the peak, teasing me, the light puffs of his breath caressing my skin.

His hooded gaze catches mine. "But your tits aren't your best feature."

"They're not?"

"Nope. Your ass." His voice dips lower on the last word, rumbly and drawn out with heat, conviction, and a touch of—oh my gosh—reverence. "It's so nice and round and firm, I just want to bite it."

Suddenly I get it. Because, yeah. "I want to bite yours too," I whisper. Just thinking about his cuppable ass and how good it looks in jeans has me flushing with heat again. He must sense the shift in me, because while he's still grinning, his eyes have pinned mine, and they're intense.

I pull in a sharp breath at what I see in their depths—raw need, mixed with tenderness.

He grabs the back of his shirt, and I sit up and help with removal. Mainly I just want to skim my hands up the contoured muscles of his chest and then up his biceps and forearms as we clear the fabric from his head and arms. His scent—masculine, clean—surrounds me and gets me even more worked up. I didn't know *scent* could be such a turn-on. Basically, anything associated with Aiden is a turn-on.

He pulls his wallet from his back pocket, thumbs out a condom, and tosses the wallet next to us, holding the packet in his teeth. Then he rises up on his knees, the powerful muscles of his thighs bunching with the fluid movement under the fabric of his jeans. I fall back and feast on the visual—his blunt fingers flying to the snap of his jeans, the quick tug to undo them, then pushing his jeans and boxer briefs off his hips, and his erection springing free.

I pretty much get wet right there. There's a bit of moisture down there, just sayin'.

While he's on his knees, I quickly undo my pants and shove them down. I'm still trying to kick them free of my ankles when he sweeps them away, shifts until he's kneeling between my legs, and grips himself. I watch in awe as the tendons on his forearm stand out, his whole body a sculpted study in tensed masculinity. He strokes once down his length and pinches the tip, hissing.

And suddenly I'm jealous of his friggin' hand.

I reach out, but he snatches the condom packet from his teeth. "Hands beside your head. Jesus, Jane, I swear, if you touch me right now, I'll come all over you." Desperation laces his voice.

That outcome shouldn't turn me on, but it does. Oh, it *does*. I'm also past worrying about what turns me on. Aiden turns me on, period. And I don't care what I might say or do either—I feel free to be myself with him.

I obey, though, and slowly draw my hands back, the sheets brushing coolly against my skin, until my fingers graze my ears.

He tears open the package and deftly rolls on the condom, his forearms and biceps bunching with his efficient movements. He leans down, resting his weight on one hand next to my shoulder, the other hand guiding himself.

All the tension and anticipation that's been building ever since we sat at the picnic table and realized we both wanted more seems to ratchet higher now, the moment weighty with significance.

He slides the crown through my already slick folds, the slide a delicious feeling. I widen my legs and arch, cool air kissing me down there, because God, I can't wait for him to slide inside, to fill me up. It's an ache, this need for him to be inside me.

His jaw clenched, he strokes up and down my cleft with the head of his cock and then circles my clit, pressing with just the right amount of pressure. Down again and back up to do a tight circle.

Oh my God, my whole being is concentrated in that tight bundle of nerves, and I think my legs are thrashing, and I'm mumbling something, but I have no idea what. I do know this—I'm staring down my body, seeing him stretched out above the length of me, all his muscles tightly defined, and his hand pushing that thick cock of his through my folds and teasing my clit, up down around, and then a tight little circle, and then I'm grabbing his wrist that's by my shoulder and bucking as an orgasm sings through me, its notes pulsing, beautiful, but not enough.

He moans. "Jesus. That was hot."

I roll my head back, eyes clamping shut, because that rumbly, silky voice curls right through me, prolonging the pleasure, amplifying the pulse. The sensual waves are just receding, relaxing and releasing my muscles from their hold, when he thrusts, fast and hard, into me.

Delicious invasion. I gasp and snap my eyes open. He's stretched above me, his weight on his elbows, and his head back, eyes closed, his expression almost pained.

Instead of whipping my legs around him like my body urges, I stroke my hands down his broad back, feeling each bump along his spine. I reach the little indentation at the base, and then graze my fingers up the curve and cup that firm butt.

His gaze finds mine, hooded but intense. I grip him. All right, I *squeeze* his butt cheeks, okay? And watch in fascination as it makes his abs clench. I do it again, this time pulling him down further, grinding him against that bundle of nerves. Just having him inside me, his heated length stretching and filling me this way, I almost don't want him to move—I want to savor it so much. But there's an insistent need to move too. My heart wants to get all soul-connecting mushy, while my body's like, c'mon with the friction already, dangit.

I tell my body to pipe down. Because this *is* a moment. Oh my God, is it. And I *do* want to savor it.

He does too. I can tell. His eyes are full of it, though I think we're still too scared to voice it just yet. It's still so new. I'm horrified to discover I'm about to cry. I swallow and blink, tamping that feeling down.

Never breaking eye contact, he puts his weight on one elbow and smoothes a hand up along my thigh, the skim of his palm along my skin raising goosebumps in its wake. Up my hip and waist he goes, until he gently cups my breast. He's too tall to reach it with his mouth, but he tweaks the tip and slowly massages my breast.

"Jane." His voice is low, gravelly.

"Yes?" I tear my gaze from how his long, talented fingers tease and pinch.

His eyes search mine. "I'm going to start moving."

"Yes, please," I whisper.

He chuckles, his gaze still intent on mine. He rotates his hips, hitting me in just the right spot with his pubic bone. I swear to God, I feel as if I'm close to coming again.

"And I'm not going to stop."

"Please don't."

He pinches my nipple, and I gasp.

"If I may continue?" He raises both eyebrows in question.

I squeeze his butt again and roll my hips, and when he closes his eyes and hisses? That feminine power surges through me.

"Yeah, fuck." His Adam's apple bobs. "I'm telling you, Jane. I'm going to last about three thrusts. Five at the most. But I'm going to do my damnedest to make each one count. I want you to feel each and every one, okay? Feel how I fit inside you, feel how full I make you, and I want you to understand on each of those thrusts, how much you *do* get me worked up. So much so, I'm not going to be able to last long with my new fucking girlfriend."

I know it shouldn't, but that word melts me a little more. He's evidently not too scared to voice that much about what's potentially going on here with us.

"Yeah?"

"Yeah." He eases out, his butt slipping from my hands—*just* out of reach—and then he rocks slowly back in with an insistent push right at the end. For emphasis. "Feel that, Jane?"

"Yes," I whisper and grip his backside again.

The hand at my breast moves down to my hip, and he drags out. All of my thoughts and feelings narrow down to the searing heat of him leaving me, the wonderful slick friction of it, and then the slight ache of being almost empty of him, before he glides slowly back in. Filling me.

And as he does, I understand what he's trying to tell me. I feel his thrust and how it makes me feel, but I watch and listen and feel what it does to him too. Oh God. Tears well in my eyes again.

I feel powerful *and* beautiful. Wanted.

"I haven't started yet," he says on a gasp.

"You haven't?"

"No." He shakes his head. "This is me manfully trying to draw this out a little longer before I lose control and start pounding into you."

I clench around him at his frank words and the visual that forms in my mind's eye, and he groans.

"You're a talker, aren't you?" I whisper on a half-laugh.

"Yeah, surprises me too. Never have before. I think I'm stalling."

I smile and squeeze his butt cheeks. "I think you are too."

I push my hips up a bit.

His nostrils flare on an inhale, and the edge of his mouth curls up. "Touch yourself."

A jolt of trepidation and excitement tightens my stomach. With my past boyfriends, I had the distinct impression that doing this insulted their prowess. Like it was an indictment. But this is Aiden.

"Like this?" Good God, is that my voice? It's all low and husky. I skim my hand up his back and some instinct has me bring my fingers to his mouth. I brush a fingertip along that fat part of his lower lip that drives me wild. Impossibly, his eyes darken, and he sucks my fingers. Desire coils tighter at the sight. I bring my hand down to where we're joined. He breaks my gaze, following my movement. My fingers probe my swollen clit and the cool wetness from my fingers touches me. I gasp.

"Five strokes is a fucking pipe dream," he groans, gripping my hip tighter. "Yeah, like that, baby. I'm going to come fast and hard, and I want you coming too."

His words make me tremble, and my fingers stroke hard, chasing the need. He grips my hip, slides out and slams into me.

"Aiden!"

The thrust feels like possession, like desire, like…everything.

I spread my legs wider, one hand skipping up and down his muscled back trying to find purchase, the other working my clit.

And then he snaps. His hips are frenzied thrusts, pounding into me over and over. And now instead of it being what I feel, or seeing how he feels, it's an *us* thing as emotion builds with tension on each stroke. My back pulls tight as an orgasm bursts so hard through me that I'm clamping down hard on his butt and my mouth drops open as if I'm going to scream but no words come out. And the pleasure keeps building and spilling, building and spilling, as I ride his frantic thrusts. He captures my mouth with his, our tongues tangle, and with a grunt he thrusts one more time. His whole body goes rigid, and he gasps into my mouth.

I whip my legs up tight around his hips, my arms around his back, as he pulses and kicks deep inside me, making me shudder again with another climax.

He collapses against me, holding our sweaty bodies tightly together, and I relish how he feels against me, inside me.

I can't lift my arms. Seriously. I'm…yeah. Can't move. But who cares, right?

I don't know what our future brings, but for once I feel the courage to see.

23

Jane

"So you and Aiden, huh?" Pepper stands from the hotel lobby's chair.

The men's game is in less than an hour, so we're heading there now. It's afternoon, and I haven't seen Aiden since our early morning wake-up sex-a-palooza. Before he left to meet the team at some god-awful time, he had the strangest request—don my pj's. His eyes flared with heat when I groggily complied, and he promptly divested me of them, leading to the sheet-scorching sex.

I cinch my messenger bag over my shoulder and grin. "Yeah."

She nods. "He seems like a really nice guy. He owns the Alligator's Butt, right?"

"Yep." And I like that she sees him differently than Claire. Last night, I texted Claire to let her know I was here, since I knew she was set to fly in with the women's team. I was worried she'd want to meet up, but she texted back to say she was going straight to bed. We're meeting her at the game.

Last night in the elevator, Pepper and Luke were the first to witness my relationship with Aiden. I don't know what flowed through me when Luke started his lecture, but I think I was feeling the weight of not only my guilt in misjudging Aiden, but also how much Claire had misread him, and I couldn't stand it anymore.

Pepper and I spend the short drive to the fields finding out about each other and how we met the guys. "Claire seems totally cool," she says when she learns Claire's my bestie. "I can't wait to see the women's team play."

Claire plays camogie, the girl's version of hurling, but they don't have a full team, so they're doing an exhibition match with a couple of other not-full teams to get in some game time. Their game is after the guys' match.

Soon we're pulling into the sports complex where the playoffs are being held. The parking lot is crowded, so we don't find a spot in the shade.

She jumps out of the car. "Ready to see some hot men play a rough sport?"

"How dangerous is it?" I have no clue about this sport. I just know it has a ball and a stick.

She shrugs and heads toward the fields, and I follow. "On par with rugby, I'd say. It's confusing as hell, so don't panic that the rules seem all over the place. But the basics are there's a round ball, they can hit it with a stick, or with their hands—"

"Ouch."

She glances at me. "Yeah. Some of those balls have been clocked at over a hundred miles an hour, and they *catch* them in their bare hands."

I stop walking. "At that speed?"

"Well, no, I suspect those are hit with the stick, but still. Anyway, three points if it makes it into the goal net, or one point if it's over the goal bar and between the posts."

"Like a field goal."

"You got it."

By now we're filing through the gate with other spectators, and I see Claire just beyond, waiting on us.

She comes up and gives me a big hug. "I'm so glad you could come."

"Me too." After Aiden left, I spent the morning lounging

by the pool, reading and finishing up my journal. This time, I pasted in all the pictures of Aiden, daring to give shape to what's going on between us. It's *my* journal. Not Claire's.

It was scary, the hope embodied in that action, though.

Claire and Pepper greet each other, and I turn to Pepper. "Meet you in the stands?"

"You bet. Don't dawdle too much, though. Our men are going to want to come by for a good luck kiss." She waves and angles toward the stands.

Claire rounds on me. "Hold. The. Effing. Door. Our men?" She's got a you-go-girl grin for me, which I know is about to disappear.

My face heats. "About that." I pull out the journal and hand it over. "I had a great time on the trip."

She laughs as she takes it, opening it to the first page. "Must have if you met someone on it. I *knew* this would be good for you." She fist pumps and starts flipping pages. And then she pauses once she gets to the Bongoland entry, because now the photos include Aiden. She flips through faster and takes in the ones at the end showing us at the earlier stops. The ones I'd left out.

"The Turd? He was on this trip with you?" She snaps the journal shut. "What the hell, Jane? This was to help you move past him." She actually looks as if she's about to go into Mama-Bear mode.

I hold up a hand, the same feeling of injustice filling me like it did in the elevator last night. "Stop right there. First of all, he's not a turd. That was your nickname for him, and I went along. Also? You're the one who read way more into what happened and thought I was all broken up over him. I was crushed, yes, when you punctured my image of him that morning. But then, I don't know, I just accepted the outcome."

She shakes her head. "You got more into your shell. You just didn't see it."

I shrug. Maybe she's right. But that's behind me now. "You misjudged him."

"But—"

"You did. Trust me, okay?"

She looks hard at me, her eyes searching mine. She chews her lower lip. "Okay. I just hate to see you get hurt."

"I'm a big girl."

She hands me back my journal. "You're right. I'm sorry."

Claire's a strange enigma. She's full-on tomboy. She probably couldn't care less whether her nails are manicured or not. Sees it, and other girly things, as a waste of time. But she's got a protective, mothering instinct that is fierce to witness at times.

We start walking to the stands. "So have you seen Conor yet?"

Her step falters, but she recovers fast. "Why would you ask that?"

Payback. "Oh, so we're still pretending we don't have the hots for that Irishman?"

She waves a hand in front of her and makes a *pfth* sound. "Crazy talk."

"God. You're in such denial."

"Whatever. Let's get you a beer, okay? I can't have one, so you're drinking one for me."

I laugh. "Ooookaaay."

Soon I have a beer in hand, the side of the clear plastic cup already wet with condensation, and we make our way up the aisle of steps to where Pepper's sitting with a small group. One of them's Aiden, watching me with a huge grin on his face, and my heart does a little skippy dance.

Then my face heats just thinking about where I'd last seen that impish grin. This morning, between my legs.

I have no time to even worry how he's going to play this in front of everyone because he's bounding down the aisle, his steps clanging a staccato beat on the metal. He yanks me up against him. I squeal, because a) he took me by surprise, b) he's already a little sweaty, and c) my beer sloshed onto my hand.

He gives me a big huge smack on the lips and sets me

down, and I know I've got the dopiest grin on my face. I don't even care.

Luke treads down the steps and slaps his shoulder. "Game time, lover boy."

Aiden ignores him. He holds my chin. "You'll be here after the game, right?"

"Of course. We need to celebrate your win, don't we?"

He gives a quick nod with a mock-serious face. "Damn straight." Another quick peck, and he follows the rest of the guys onto their side of the field.

The taste and heat of him lingers on my mouth, and as I watch him flow into interacting with his team, I'm struck by a new feeling. Normally, I'd feel so out of my element here. Hello, I'm at a sporting event! But…it doesn't matter. For once, I'm in a social situation outside of my comfort zone and…I'm fine. More than fine.

Aiden

Holy fucking shit. We might win this thing. *If* I can make this penalty goal. There's only a few minutes on the clock, and we're one point behind.

I'm winded, my legs are burning, but never have I felt more pumped. As if I can do anything. Part of the feeling is due to a certain person watching me in the stands. But that's not all of it. I think, up till now, I never really believed we could win. Or believed it mattered.

I joined and agreed to take it seriously, but I didn't actually *believe*. Let's just say I thought a lot of it was wishful thinking that also keeps me in shape. But the discipline and hard work Conor and Luke insisted on from day one are paying off.

Since I can't hit the *sliotar* past this point, I take it back a couple of yards to give myself running room, while I tell myself to calm the fuck down—my heart's pounding like a mofo.

The team ranges behind me as five of their guys line the goal box. Luke and Conor nod, and Paolo's grinning like a fiend. Because they all know what the opposing team doesn't. Sure, I'm predictable on the field as a point scorer, but when I have a chance like this—a controlled bat—I go for the goal. Plus a point will only put us in overtime. A goal will win it.

I set the *sliotar* on the field, adjusting it a smidge, and jog back a few steps. I turn. And run. Everything narrows down to the sound of my breathing and my feet hitting the grass. I slip my hurley under the *sliotar* and fling it up. My arm muscles sing as they pull back and then that jolt when I make a perfect connection. *Smack!*

Sure enough, most of them were poised for a jump in an attempt to block a point, and that pretty little ball drives hard into a gap in the lower left pocket of the goal.

It all happens so fast. I'm still running forward from the momentum of my bat, but at that sweet sight, I spin around and pump a fist into the air. I may have also given a shout. Hey, it was wicked, and right now I'm feeling like Superman. Hell, maybe I'm Supermouth here too, cuz I'm screaming myself hoarse.

There's still time on the clock, but there's no fucking way that wasn't the winning shot.

Their goalie bats it down field, but sure enough, they don't get far when the whistle blows.

Game. We did it!

Then a bunch of sweaty teammates smother me, and we do a jar-bounce-hug in one giant ball off the field.

What a fucking high. I got the girl *and* the winning goal.

Jane

THEY WON!

The last several minutes we've been acting like scream-freaks. Ever since Aiden made his run down field and got the penalty shot. And while that totally sounds as if I have a handle on how the game's played, that'd be a big fat no. But the rush to stand, the happy grins, and frenzied clapping has gotta be good.

Pepper confirms it. "We won!"

We make a mad dash down the bleachers to greet the team. It's just five of us cheering, but we feel mighty in our support.

We reach the ground, and Aiden's gaze homes in on mine. He pushes away from the guys pounding his back and runs to me. How the heck does he still have the energy? I'm exhausted *for* him. He grabs me in a bear hug, lifts me off the ground, and plants one right on my lips. He's now full-on sweaty, but this time I don't squeak.

The energy of the game still vibrates through him. An adrenaline rush for me by osmosis.

"We did it," he says between breaths.

I give him another kiss. "No, *you* did it." I squeeze him tight, loving that I can do this, that I'm so comfortable and not second-guessing everything I say or do.

"Shh, let's keep that to ourselves, okay? Team spirit and all."

I laugh, but just then the others walk by and each one gives him either a slap on his shoulder or butt and says, "You did it, man," or "You the man," or "Way to go. Now, to celebrate!" Each and every one, he fervently brushes off the praise.

After the last goes by, he touches his forehead to mine and whispers against my lips, "Got a present for you."

He's hard against my stomach. I snort and push into it a little. "I don't think that's something we can unwrap right now."

He throws his head back with a full-on laugh, and the vibrations tease me all up and down my body, flush against his. His teammates, and Pepper and Claire, look on in wonder. They're not even pretending they're not watching.

"Hang on." He disengages from me, hustles to his duffel bag, and returns. From its depths, he lifts up a hot pink gift bag.

"Oh! A real present."

He chuckles, grabs my hip, and gives me a little shake. "Yes. A real present. Ran to the store after the team meeting."

He laces our fingers together and tugs me up and over to a row, away from everyone still lingering.

I take the bag, and we sit down next to each other, the metal seat hot from the sun. The gift's definitely from a specialty store, because the tissue paper is all fancy and done with perfect peaks.

I pull the paper out and peer inside.

And my whole body flushes with heat. I swear to God, I clench right there on the metal seat.

Because at the bottom of the bag is a hot pink vibrator.

Aiden drapes an arm over my shoulder and pulls me up tight to his side. His lips brush my ear. "This is to replace the one you burnt." His voice is low with a touch of gravel, which has me tingling all over and wishing I *could* unwrap his other "present."

"Thought it'd be more…versatile than a dildo. I'm looking forward to us playing with that."

Oh God. I shudder all over. I bite my lip and glance up at him. "I can't wait," I whisper.

He groans and shifts on the bench. "I can't either. Fuck. But—" He plucks the bag from me and sets it to the side. Then he turns to me, and his face is completely serious. He slides his hands across my jaw until he's cradling my head, his gaze boring into mine.

You know what else I love? That being under such intense scrutiny doesn't make me squirm.

"The two of us," he rumbles. "We're going to have a lot of adventures together."

My heart leaps. "We are."

He brushes his lips across mine. "Inside and outside of the bedroom."

Yes.

And as he deepens the kiss as much as we dare in public, a strange feeling suffuses me, as if I'm glowing from the rightness, the happiness, filling me as our tongues tangle, my hands gripping his jersey, his hands gently holding me.

And while this happy glow is amazing in and of itself, there's an added significance. Because, let's face it, we're talking about me here.

This glow, it feels as if it can be seen by everyone—like a beacon—and that makes me happy too. Like I'm here, world. I'm here, I'm happy, and I think I'm in love.

THE END

AUTHOR'S NOTE

This won't be as long as my usual, but just a quick note to say, yes, each spot they visited is real, y'all! Including the Potty Chair!

ACKNOWLEDGEMENTS

I'D LIKE TO thank the following folks who read early versions and helped me make this a better story! Jami Gold, Shaila Patel (who read it twice). You guys helped me to not only craft a better story, but also helped in the cheerleading department too. Thank you!

I'd also like to thank several of my readers who also read early versions and gave me helpful feedback: Megan and Deb, thank you!

My editors Gwen Hayes, Erynn Newman, and Julie Glover had my back again, which I appreciate so much.

I'd also like to thank some of my friends, some from my high school days, who suggested stops for Aiden and Jane. I appreciate it! And special thanks to Julie Lapides, who went farther and sent me awesome pics of Solomon's Castle and provided insight into that awesome location that helped me bring it to life. Much appreciated, Julie!

To my friend Cortlandt for giving me insight into owning a bar. Your idea of what could go wrong for Aiden was perfect and without you, I wouldn't have known about Florida's weird liquor laws!

And to Christopher Cox who answered questions about what it's like to have Jane's job. Though a lot of that information didn't make it into the book, it helped me get a better picture of her.

I also want to thank the members of my facebook fan group for their help and support!

I'd also like to thank my facebook and twitter friends who are always willing to answer questions I pose, whether it's about writing, or character ideas, or an opinion sought

And finally to my family, who have always believed in me and make it possible for me to pursue writing.

ABOUT THE AUTHOR

ANGELA QUARLES IS a RWA RITA® Winner and *USA Today* bestselling author of time travel, steampunk, and now contemporary romance. Her steampunk, *Steam Me Up, Rawley*, was named Best Self-Published Romance of 2015 by *Library Journal* and *Must Love Chainmail* won the 2016 RITA® Award in the paranormal category, the first indie to win in that category. Angela loves history, folklore, and family history. She decided to take this love of history and her active imagination and write stories of romance and adventure for others to enjoy. When not writing, she's either working at the local indie bookstore or enjoying the usual stuff like gardening, reading, hanging out, eating, drinking, chasing squirrels out of the walls, and creating the occasional knitted scarf.

Photo by Keyhole Photography

She has a B.A. in Anthropology and International Studies with a minor in German from Emory University, and a Masters in Heritage Preservation from Georgia State University. She was an exchange student to Finland in high school and studied abroad in Vienna one summer in college.

Find Angela Quarles Online:
www.angelaquarles.com
@angelaquarles
Facebook.com/authorangelaquarles
Mailing list: www.angelaquarles.com/join-my-mailing-list

Love Angela's writing style?

Try her time travel series following a modern woman to Regency England!

Purchase *Must Love Breeches* at your favorite retailer in ebook or print format

She's finally met the man of her dreams—too bad he lives in a different century!

A devoted history buff finds the re-enactment of a pre-Victorian ball in London a bit boring…until a mysterious artifact sweeps her back in time to the real event, and into the arms of a compelling British lord.

Isabelle Rochon can't believe it when she finds herself in the reality of 1830's London high society. She's thrilled to witness events and people she's studied. But she may also have to survive without modern tools or career—unless she can find a way to return to her time. And then there's Viscount Lord Montagu, a man whose embrace curls her toes, but who has a dangerous agenda of his own.

Lord Phineas Montagu is on a mission to avenge his sister, and he'll stop at nothing, including convincing an alluring stranger to pose as his respectable fiancé. He's happy to repay her by helping her search for her stolen calling card case that brought her back in time. But he doesn't bargain for the lady being his intellectual match—or for the irresistible attraction that flames between them.

They're both certain they know what they want, but as passion flares, Phineas must keep both himself and Isabella safe from unseen opponents, and she must choose when and where her heart belongs. Can they ever be together for good?

Made in the USA
Columbia, SC
07 November 2017